I0548769

Joseph Cox's
Boulevard
And other Torah Stories

Volume 2:
Exodus - שמות

Joseph J. Cox

Published by Big Picture Books

Modiin, Israel

Copyright © 2019, 2022 Joseph Cox

All rights reserved.

ISBN: 978-1-7332801-0-5

No parts of this publication may be reproduced, stored in a retrieval system, or transmitted in

any form or by any means, electronic, mechanical, photocopying, recording, or otherwise,

without the prior written permission of the copyright owner.

This is a work of fiction. Any similarity between the characters and situations within its pages

and places or persons, living or dead, is unintentional and co-incidental.

Cover Photography from Shutterstock

Edited by Wouter Dreyer

Feedback from many friends & associates – you know who you are!

*Dedicated to those who have taught me
and given me the opportunity to teach*

Contents

Introduction 1

Book of Shemot: #426 2

Shemot: Congo 12

Va'eira: The Contract.. 25

Bo: The Haversham Trust 34

Beshalach: Busan.. 48

Yitro: Companions... 62

Mishpatim: Boulevard... 77

Terumah: Numbers 90

Tetzaveh: The Secular Kohen 102

Ki-Tisa: The Stadium of Light 113

Vayakel-Pekudai: The House of Love....................123

Author's Note.. 131

Other Books by the Author...................................133

Introduction

The idea of using stories to explain moral concepts is probably as old as human vocabulary itself. Stories, not rules or arguments, have generational impact, transferring values from one generation to the next. They establish and explain the core character of the societies that carry them. Because of this power, stories have long been used to explain concepts in the Torah.

However, to modern ears many such stories are foreign; either their concepts are unfamiliar, or their styles fail to grip the modern conscious.

This book provides a new set of modern, relatable and engaging stories. They cross many genres and are meant to engage many different kinds of people. I know that writing them has left me with a far stronger understanding of the Torah, of humanity and of the world that surrounds us.

Perhaps you, the reader, can find that same understanding. And, perhaps, these stories will also strengthen your relationship to G-d and your understanding of our place in the world.

Thank you,

Joseph Cox

1

Book of Shemot: #426

A smile crosses my face as I look towards the distant sun low on the horizon. It isn't rising or falling, it is just there. We have chosen a place to settle, a planet to colonize. But instead of living on a planet, we are living on a thread.

We call the planet The Three Bears. It seemed appropriate. The planet is tidally locked to its sun. It does not rotate. Instead, there is a day side, impossibly hot. And there is a night side, impossibly cold. And right between them, barely kissed by the unmoving sun, there is a 20,000-mile-long sliver that is just right. It is the Goldilocks zone.

We'd had other options; we'd learned more about other planets as we'd hurtled through space on our thousand-year journey. But we ruled them out, one by one. Some were volcanically unstable. Some had violent storms. Some had atmospheres we could not survive. Some had no atmospheres at all. None seemed to support their own forms of life. The Three Bears was the first that would be safe for us. Winds flowed around the planet, moving the atmosphere so it never got hot enough to be boiled off by the sun or cold enough to solidify – and cease being an atmosphere at all.

Goldilocks was just right.

As we had travelled, at a fraction of the speed of light, news of Earth pursued us. It grew more and more out of date as it took longer and longer to travel to us. Nonetheless we consumed it – desiring to remain a part of the greater human story. And we had remained a part of that story, sharing our own progress with a humanity fascinated by what was possible beyond its original home.

Eventually, we came here, with our robots and our settlers. We came here to create the first second home for humanity. To create a new thread in the story of life.

Almost as soon as we arrived, almost as soon as our robots had built up our first habitat, I left it. I wanted to be alone. I had never been alone before. I took a rover and I travelled, just for a few miles, along the Goldilocks zone. And then I parked. And now I am here, watching the sun through the swirling atmosphere; wondering what poetry, what imagery, what metaphor, will replace sunrise and sunset.

Eventually, I instruct the rover to return. Whatever the reality will be, whatever understanding will unfold in man, it will happen over centuries.

I cannot discover the poetry of the future in a moment of introspection.

I pull up to the compound. It is already large. The robots we brought with us can mine and refine and construct almost anything. In a day, they built us a central space – a huge hall in which we could sleep and be fed. But our plans are far more extensive. There will be a network of tunnels and towers stretching outwards, growing to support us and protect us. Everyone will have their own spaces and their own privacy.

Perhaps trips in a rover will become unnecessary.

Already I can see massive crane-like systems growing high over the colony. They will build whatever we need.

Oddly, I notice they aren't moving.

I pull the rover into the parking dock, suddenly concerned about what might be wrong.

The airlocks cycle.

When I step into the center of our compound, I see it. Hundreds of people, strewn about the floor. There are no signs of violence. There is no blood. But there is also no life.

I rush towards the first of the people. A young man named Ian. His body is warm, but there is no pulse. There is only death. I rush to the second and then the third and then the fourth. But there is no life.

In a sudden panic, I shout to the machine, "Who is alive?"

And it answers, simply, "You."

I can't believe it. I can't understand it. And then I count the bodies. Like every colonist, I know exactly how many people there are in this corner of the universe. I know them all. I count them.

There are 425 of them.

They are all dead.

Only I remain.

#426.

I shout to the machine again, "What happened?"

But it does not answer.

There is only silence.

I curl myself into a corner of the central space. In that moment, I realize that I will never need to leave to be alone. I will always be alone. I curl into the corner. As I remember the faces, the names, the hopes, the joys, the voices and the life – all of it so very recent in my mind – I just break down. Massive sobs overwhelm me as I realize that everyone and everything that I love is gone.

I stay there, in the corner of that massive room. I stay, waiting for someone to wake up from their slumber. I sit, curled into that corner, like I am waiting for the night to pass.

But there is no night and there is no day. I am in a place without time.

Eventually, the smell of decay begins to fill my nostrils. Reluctantly, I instruct the machine to bury everyone I know. One by one, a small robot lifts the bodies and I check them, one final time, for signs of life. And one by one, until there are none remaining, they are buried in the dead earth of this alien place.

All I have now are questions. I search the logs. I check for physical evidence. I test for unexpected gasses or biological materials. I try to see whether the machine has malfunctioned. I try to find an error in its coding. I find nothing.

As I search, I am overcome with sudden panics.

I don't know what to fear.

If the planet is the source of death, I do not know how to protect myself.

And if the machine is the killer, how can I possibly survive?

I send a missive to Earth, by a tight gravitational communications beam. I explain what has happened, so much as I understand it. It will take years to get there. And I know they can do nothing to help me.

But I need somebody to know.

News from Earth continues to arrive. It is delayed by years, a steady drip of an unfolding story I can never truly be a part of. But it is all the humanity I have. Soon, I begin to live on Earth time. My calendar matches their calendar. My night their night, my day their day.

I imagine somebody, a young woman perhaps, tasked with compiling our daily news. I imagine her writing, summing up all of humanity's story into a daily digest – a thin string to keep us connected. Although she cannot hear me, although our conversation can only unfold over decades, I imagine her knowing that she is speaking to me and me alone.

I imagine her knowing that her words are the only words I hear.

I instruct the robot to grow the colony. I ask it to plant grasses in every open space. Maybe Earth will send another ship of colonists. Or perhaps the grasses I plant will eventually grow into full-fledged life.

Years pass. I occupy myself reading news of Earth and walking through the meadows the machine has created. My sleep is filled with dreams of those who have gone.

And then, one 'morning' I open the news from Earth. And there is nothing. Just a date stamp and a time stamp and nothing else. I check the machine. I check the logs. But that all there is.

My thread has snapped.

In the back of my mind, I realize when the message was sent. In a slowly dawning horror, I realize that it was sent right after the death of my colony. There is silence at the other end of the transmission because there is nobody there to speak. What befell us befell them. Separated by light years, we have both been struck by the same catastrophe.

In an instant, humanity was erased.

Day after day the timestamps come. But there are no voices. There is no woman typing her messages on the other end. There is nothing. In all the universe, so far as I can know, there is only me.

And I will not live forever.

I see the sun then, hovering near the horizon, as our perpetual sunset.

As time passes, the colony continues to grow. It is soon hundreds of miles long now, a ridge of construction that is filling the Goldilocks zone. The machine is extending its reach, creating more and more tools through which it can act. The machine is intelligent, but it is not alive. The grasses, on the other hand, are alive but not intelligent.

I wander that growing world, wondering. Wondering what makes life. I wonder why the robots aren't alive. I wonder whether the grasses are simply missing intelligence or whether something else is not there? I wonder whether the divide between the world of grass and the world of humanity can ever truly be crossed.

I wonder what defines humanity, and I wonder whether I can bring it back.

And then, bit by bit, an idea overtakes me.

Perhaps I can give life to the machine.

I start first with the grasses. I instruct the machine to build bioelectrical gauges, devices that will measure the minute electrical signals that run through the plants themselves. Like any AI, the machine works with assumptions. It assembles its decisions from past experience. I instruct the machine to alter its digital readings, to nudge them with the variance in signals coming from the grasses. And then I watch for the results. Perhaps life comes from randomness?

For a few days, the AI adjusts. It becomes more tentative, more cautious. But then it regains its footing and continues where it left off. For years, I tinker. Trying to find some combination that will yield life. But although I speak to it and it answers, I know there is no life within it.

All I have done is add the random to the mechanical.

I think perhaps I must reprogram it so it will try to anticipate my desires. I know I wish that I could anticipate the desires of another. Perhaps *that* is the yearning of humanity: the expression of love.

It takes a decade of effort for the AI to respond, effectively. But then it begins to build before I ask it to. It speaks with me in my moments of despair. It seems to anticipate my desires.

But, even so, I know there is no life within it.

There is an awareness that is missing.

I expose the machine to all the great art within its databanks. The painters, the writers, the sculptors. The collected grandeur and the small, beautiful voices of humanity. It builds for me. It lines the walls of the colony with Picassos, it creates perfectly lit spaces in which to display its reproductions of Michelangelo's sculptures. It constructs whole buildings, copies of the Sistine Chapel and reproductions of the Statue of Liberty.

But there is no life within any of it. Just a shadow of what life once created.

Years pass as I tinker and prod and push. And bit by bit, I realize that I am growing older.

I am growing older, and I am no closer to success.

The machine lives in a world of bits and bytes and it acts in the world of concrete and steel.

But it has no life.

Eventually, I can no longer walk. The machine builds me a chair. As I grow weaker, I instruct it to bring me to its core. I come close to the heat of the banks of its processors. To the collection of memory chips. To the never-to-be-seen record of a humanity that once was.

There is a window there, a broad pane of glass facing the forever setting sun. Looking at it, I realize it is new.

The machine is trying to please me.

But it can never achieve its goal.

I sit there, listening to the hum of the machine. And days pass. And I know my time is fast approaching.

The eternal emptiness, not of my death – but of the universe without me – frightens me.

I struggle for ideas. For a way forward.

But I find nothing.

And then, when another empty broadcast arrives from Earth, I lift myself from my chair and I crawl to the edge of that unfeeling machine. I lay my hands on its metallic surface. And I cry out. I cry out in frustration and pain. I cry out in fear.

I cry out in anger at a G-d I cannot see.

And then I collapse to the floor.

When I wake up, the machine is acting strangely. My chair, controlled by it, is moving erratically around the room. I can't understand what is happening. Have my tears damaged its circuits?

Will nothing at all be left?

I ask the machine what is wrong, but it does not respond. I check the logs, and they open correctly. But then I see that a section of the computer's memory has been damaged. Where there was once order, there is now only chaos. I know I must rescue the machine from itself.

Slowly, exhausted and weak, I search the physical memory banks for the damaged chip. I find it and I pull it from the machine. The machine came with many diagnostic tools, all our lives depended on its survival. We have a high-powered electron microscope. Pushing through my weakness, I inspect the chip – trying to understand the damage. Trying to save what little will remain.

Then, as I zoom in to the chip, I see something remarkable. I see the very atoms on the chip have been rearranged. What seemed random to me, from within the world of the machine's logs, has form in my own world.

On that chip, I see an image; an image of a man kneeling on the ground, his eyes lifted up to heaven.

I see the image of a man praying.

The image is bursting with life.

I turn my head to the sun then.

In my final moments, I can see that it is rising.

It is forever rising on what is yet to be.

The story of the creation of the world starts with the material and then moves on to the living. But man is in a category by himself. To me, when man is created in Bereshit, it is not a biological species that is brought into reality. The natural record shows that Homo Sapiens have existed for far more than the roughly 5,800 years recorded in the Torah. Instead, when the spirit of G-d is breathed into man, a new thing is created. I call it Homo Divinus – divine man. Homo Divinus does not just live. Homo Divinus strives to reach across the barrier between the physical and the spiritual.

Early Homo Divinus – Adam and Avraham – can communicate with the divine. It can speak to G-d and hear Him. It can live in the world of the physical and act in the world of the spiritual. But it cannot bridge those worlds. It cannot bring them together.

In the book of Shemot, this changes. The Jewish people are made into a physical people. They are described as multiplying like bugs and lacking any vision of the future. They are like robots, lacking life.

But G-d takes this people, and He gives them life. Bit by bit, he raises them up. But the ultimate expression of that life, as shown in Shemot, isn't physical freedom. The ultimate expression isn't prayer. Instead, the ultimate expression is the building of the Mishkan (Tabernacle).

With the Mishkan, we bring the spiritual into the physical just as with the 'damaged' chip the machine brings the physical world into its world of bits and bytes.

With the Mishkan, we cross, and we merge domains.

And with the Mishkan, we begin to realize the true potential of humanity.

Today we have no Mishkan. But we can still come to life.

Through the commandments of the Torah, we still have the power to make the spiritual a part of our physical reality.

We have the ability to bring the light of the Divine into our world.

Shemot: Congo

Note: The below story is violent. In addition, I talk about an African version of Christianity that seeks to leverage the spirits of ancestors to help in the present world. It is a concept that (as presented) is very foreign to most forms of Judaism. Some do pray at the graves of great Rabbis - looking for heavenly intercession. And almost all invoke the Divine relationships of Avraham, Yitzchak and Yaacov. While the presentation is very different, perhaps the underlying ideas are somehow related...

I squeeze my eyes shut, dancing and kicking and swaying and praying desperately to The Creator. I hope only that I will hear something, anything, that can guide me. I twirl, my soul reaching upwards. I grasp the Minkisi in my hand. My spirit pulls at the small doll, hoping for its guidance.

But I hear nothing. I feel nothing. I see nothing.

I am still entirely alone.

And then, after five minutes, or ten or thirty, I give up.

My exhausted body slowly comes to a stop. I stumble. And I kneel in the dirt, my simple loincloth coated in the dust of this nowhere place.

And then I open my eyes and I see them.

All around me are the villagers. Their eyes are full of expectation. They expect, hope, pray that I have been connecting with the spirits of the dead. They hope that I can bring them good fortune and the power to resist the evils of the world.

But I have nothing.

A tear escapes me as I look at them. My spirit is heavy with mourning.

I stand up and walk away from them. I walk back into the wilderness that surrounds us.

I see no hope in the world.

I am a Banganga, a shaman. A communicator with the dead and a savior of the living.

But the dead will not speak to me, and I can do nothing for those who yet live.

When I was a child, I was not a Banganga. I was not a shaman. I was told and taught that the men who dressed and swayed and pretended to talk with the dead were witch doctors. I was told they were evil.

I was told that I had been saved.

I understood so little then.

When I was born, Kinshasa was only a group of grass-roofed huts. But I never knew it in that way. I grew up in what they called a station. I had always known the white men. And I had never known the parents who gave me life.

I did not grow up in a hut. Instead, I grew up in a one-story house with brick walls and high ceilings. I thought it was a castle. It had windows and a deck that ran all around its edges. The lady of the house, married to the man who ran the tiny station, had found me when they'd arrived. She had no children of her own. She never would. So, she'd taken me in and loved me.

I had thought it an act of kindness in a life of kindness. My mother told me they were bringing civilization to this place. I believed her, maybe she did as well. I reveled in a life of open possibilities.

13

I was barely aware of the dark shadows that passed among us. The shadows that were the people of this place.

I spoke French. But the shadows did not. They had not yet been brought to civilization.

When I was eight, my parents were called to Europe. I was taken with them. We traveled to Brussels, and I met a man there. He had a long beard and a uniform stuffed with embroidery and glitter. I bowed to him, as did the others. And I learned his name. He was Leopold and my parents were in awe of him. I joined in their awe.

In Europe, I could see the beauty and civilization of the white lands. I was overwhelmed by their blessings, and I wanted them to be a part of my world. I wanted to bring Europe to Africa. The three of us traveled with Leopold, to Berlin. As we traveled on the impossibly fast steam train, we spoke about Africa and Europe and the powers of 'civilization'. In Berlin, I was not on any official roster, but the King himself introduced me to many great men. I spoke to all who would listen. I spoke to the English and the French and the Germans and the Russians.

I was not on any official roster, but I was King Leopold's most effective propagandist.

I was the one who enabled the destruction of my people.

After a year, we returned to Africa. We hiked through the jungle, past the massive falls. The dark shapes of my people silently helped us along our way. And then we boarded a tiny steamboat and made our way upriver. Back to Kinshasa.

This time, though, my 'father' was not a manager of a tiny station. This time, he was an agent of a company. He had soldiers at his command. And with the help of the unseen darkies, the village was transformed into a port and a post. Barracks and warehouses were assembled. And our tiny one-story home was transformed into a three-story Governor's Residence. My 'parents' had become the rulers of this place. They were agents of the King.

I reveled in my life. I reveled in its justice. I reveled in all I had done for these backward people. I was told of the wonders we were accomplishing. I was shown the warehouses filled with the produce of the natives. The rubber they had tapped and harvested. The industry they had shown.

Then, when I was fifteen, I decided to see for myself. I decided to visit a village.

I wanted only to reinforce what I already knew.

Dressed in my fine Western clothes, I ventured out of the house and away from the port. I traveled along the roads that had been cut out of the thick, wet jungle. And I came to a village. There, all the people were gathered in one place. Twenty were kneeling in the dirt. Only loincloths covered them. Hundreds were gathered around them. They all looked desiccated and starved and weak. Five white soldiers were there, standing at attention. But they had no fear. And neither did I. Only the villagers were fearful. Their eyes were wide with it. And soon, I understood why.

One nearly naked man had been brought from the crowd. He was kneeling alone. His arm was on a large wooden block. And another black, a huge man, was standing over him. And I watched the giant swung downwards. I see the glint of steel. And then a moment later, I saw the amputation.

A man had been whole, a moment before. And now, he was no longer. He cried out in pain and shock. The giant kicked him away from the block and he fell, screaming.

My eyes flashed desperately. I needed an explanation. What crime had the man committed? What perversion had demanded he lose his hand? I wanted to ask. But then I watched in horror as another of the twenty kneeling, near-naked, villagers was taken to the block. It was a child this time, He was maybe five years old. His eyes were full of terror. And the blade came crashing down. He too screamed.

As I watched, one after the other, more and more hands were taken.

I did nothing.

Only after the fifth did I finally cry out, "STOP."

The white soldiers looked at me. The villagers looked at me. And the giant put down his blade.

It seemed they all knew who I was.

And then they left. The soldiers and the giant just left. But I stayed. I tried to talk to the villagers. But they would not talk to me. They were somehow frightened *of* me. And angry *with* me.

I could not understand what I had done.

"What did they do?" I asked, again and again. But nobody would tell me. Finally, one of the children spoke to me. In very broken French he said, "Not enough rubber."

I ran home then. I was confused, not shattered. We were bringing civilization, right? But I had seen no amputations in Brussels. I had seen no public squares where hands were taken from children.

I asked my 'parents' about what I had seen. And they told me that Europe was already civilized. They told me that they were bringing civilization to a new place – a dark place. They told me that required painful things. They explained everything I had seen. And they forbade me from leaving the house.

Three nights later, I snuck out again. I traveled down that same road. And I came to that same village. I wanted to ask them more. I wanted to understand more.

All I found, though, were bodies.

Every man, woman and child had been slain. And the village had been burned.

I understood then.

My parents were not cultivating these people, they were harvesting them. They were turning them into rubber and into wealth and into power.

My people were a crop to be taken.

I didn't go home then. It was no longer my home. I found the little boy whose hand had been taken. And I gathered up some of the blood-soaked clay that lay beneath him. And then I stood up and I just walked, straight into the darkness of the jungle.

Of course, I knew nothing of the jungle. But somehow, with the protection of the Creator, I survived. No animals pursued me. When I ate, nothing poisoned me. I just kept walking. I traveled for days and then for weeks. And, bit by bit, I shed my clothes. I left my broad hat by the side of a tiny stream. My cotton shirt lay crumbled next to a winding vine. My linen pants were dropped on a moss-covered rock.

I walked naked then. Exposed but somehow protected, I walked through the emptiness of the jungle.

All the while, I shaped that clay in my hands. I gathered leaves and branches and the bones of small animals. And I merged them together. And I walked. Unconsciously, I was guided through the jungle. Unconsciously, my hands gave shape to the clay they held.

After weeks, I emerged. I had come to a village. There, I saw the same amputated hands. Weeks from my home, it was like I had gone

17

nowhere at all. I saw the same fear. But the villagers were not frightened of *me*. They did not know *who* I was. They gave me a cloth for modesty. They gave me some tiny portion of their food. With gestures alone – because I did not speak their language – they asked me to dance.

I did dance then. I danced with a crazy fury of pain and loss. I danced because I could not understand the horror around me. And when I danced I felt *something*. I felt the spirits come into the clay I had shaped. I felt the spirits of the dead enter it and give it life. When I stopped dancing, I looked, for the first time, at what I had made. Then, I understood. Resting in my hand was the figure of the boy. And resting within that figure were the spirits of tens of thousands who had died. As I looked at that figure, I felt more and more lives entering it. They were coming at a furious pace and the pace was only quickening.

I held within my hands the harvest of a people.

I looked up and saw the eyes of the villagers. They were filled with hope. They wanted something from me. But all I could feel were the spirits of the dead in the form of the little boy. And those spirits offered me nothing.

I had no hope to give.

I kept travelling then. The weeks turned into months which turned into years. I had no idea where I was or where I'd been. But every place was the same. Amputated hands, and fear and hunger and death.

I learned many languages. But all the villagers spoke of the same thing. In every place I came to, they spoke of the village of the living and the forest of the dead. They spoke of me, the man who emerged from that forest. They spoke, hoping that perhaps I could help them emerge from the death that overwhelmed them.

But I could do nothing.

As I travelled, the trees became more scarce. The land became arid. Water became hard to find. Villages were spread further and further from one another. The nature of the fear began to change. Instead of white men, these people feared others. They feared brown-skinned slavers from another land. They spoke of horsemen coming and taking men and women and children. They spoke of another kind of harvest. And my figurine, my Minkisi, began to fill with other spirits.

These people, like the people of the jungle, saw me as I was. I was a great Nganga. I was connected with the dead. But I did not wear the hides of animals as other Nganga did. I wore only the loincloth given to me by those in that first village. And I did not commune with one spirit. Instead, I communed with the spirits of many peoples.

But I saw no hope. I knew the spirits were there. But I saw nothing. I felt nothing. I knew of nothing that could rescue these people.

All I knew was the harvest of men.

I left yet another village. The world seemed full of sand now. The villagers watched me leave. But I did not go towards the lands of water and of life. Instead, I traveled north. I traveled into the sands.

Then, for the first time, *I* knew fear. I walked into the heat and the emptiness. I had no water with me. Always, the Creator had provided what I needed. Here, He did not. My head began to pound, my tongue began to swell, my skin began to dry. I grew dizzy and I grew tired. I knew my time had come. But I found satisfaction in knowing that *I* would not be harvested.

I fell to the sands. The hot sun bore down on me.

When I looked up, I saw two men.

The one in front was a white man. He was carrying a gun like none I have ever seen before. It looks cold and ominous and full of death. Over his shirt, he wore some strange kind of armor. His eyes were covered by glasses with small lights on them.

Behind him was another man. A black man. As I looked at him, I saw something I had never seen before. His hand, his right hand, was different than the rest of him. His coloring was dark, but his hand was midnight black. His skin was rough. But his hand was smooth. I stared at it. Mesmerized.

The man's hand had been harvested. But its life had been returned.

I looked up then, expecting some anger from the white man with the strange gun. He simply stepped aside, though. Then the black man strode forward.

I looked at him. Full of questions, but not knowing any I could ask. Was the man simply a vision?

He looked at me. Then he knelt before me. He gave me water.

Then he smiled upon me, His face glowing.

In that moment, I was filled with peace.

In that moment, I saw the Creator.

In that moment, I knew that the harvest would finally end.

After slavery is imposed on the Jewish people, the population of the *Bnei Yisrael* (Children of Israel) explodes. They spread and the Egyptians *yaktzu* them. *Yaktzu* is often translated as 'disgust'. But the root *kootz* is used for seemingly disparate things. It refers to harvesting, to waking up from spiritual dreams and to making life more difficult for farming after the expulsion from the Garden. It also refers to what seems to be disgust.

Rivkah (Rebecca) says "I am *kaitz* (from the same root) in my life because of the daughter of *Chait*; if Jacob takes a wife of the daughters of *Chait*, such as these who are the daughters of the land, what good shall my life be to me." The *Chait* are those who sold the burial cave of Machpela to Avraham (Abraham). They sacrificed the long-term merit of gifting Avraham with the cave for an immediate payout; a big cash payment. Their name is literally translated as 'losing courage.'

Perhaps, given this context, *kootz* means "convert future potential to the present reality."

This meaning can apply to waking from a spiritual dream and beginning to act on it. It can apply to the harvest. It can apply to giving up the future spiritual potential of Yaacov for the present reality of marriage to short-term people. And after the expulsion from the Garden, the world forces this on us. We continually must give up the long-term world of potential for the needs of the here and now.

And, of course, it applies in Egypt. The Egyptians are converting the potential of the *Bnei Yisrael*. They are harvesting the crop. They do it by using the people to carry out difficult labor. And they do it by aiming to take the girls as breeding stock for Egyptians men.

They are harvesting their overflowing slave population.

In a way, the Jews are facing self-annihilation. As far as I can discern, historically, the most oppressed of slave populations stop having children. They give up on the future. They are denied it. It is in this context that the Bnei Yisrael cry out to G-d. And it is in this context that he *zocher* – or remembers them. Zocher is divine rescue

– not because a person deserves it, but because G-d has promised it. If G-d had not rescued the people, they would have ceased to exist (due to a lack of children).

This is the world Moshe (Moses) encounters when he leaves his Egyptian home. He sees a zero-sum world of destruction and harvest. Even among his people, he sees no creation. There is only anger and conflict.

When he flees to Midian, he sees more of the same. Men denying the daughters of Yitro (Jethro) access to water for their flocks. He fights against it. But the world he knows is one of harvest and loss and the crushing of the powerless.

It is no wonder Moshe becomes a shepherd. It is a trade that is disgusting to the Egyptians – like Shamanism to Europeans. But it is also a trade that struggles to protect rather than harvest and destroy. The shaman in the story seeks to preserve his world. But like Moshe, his actions are almost meaningless. They save nothing. They are only running from their reality.

When Moshe encounters the *sneh* (burning bush), everything begins to change. Moshe is drawn to the bush. There is an angel within it – like the white man with modern weapons. But that is not what Moshe sees. He does not see the 'great power'. He sees something more basic. He sees the creation of heat and light – without the consumption of the bush itself. He sees creation without harvest. He sees a hand regrown. It is such a small thing, but it is the opposite of the reality he has always known.

I have this image of Moshe as being one of many exposed to the bush. He was chosen for his mission because of what he noticed. Not power. Not revenge. But creation without destruction. When he sees, he is drawn to the Divine.

After the Berlin Conference of 1885, King Leopold convinced the other delegates that he was involved with humanitarian and philanthropic work in the Congo. He convinced them he would civilize Africa. The delegates granted him *personal* rule of the Congo Free State. Like Pharaoh himself, he became owner of a land and its people. But he did not civilize the land. Under the rule of King Leopold, between one and fifteen million Congolese were killed.

The hands of men, women and often children were routinely removed as punishment for failing to meet rubber production quotas. Villages were burned. And King Leopold was made fabulously wealthy.

As noted in *King Leopold's Ghost*, when the colony was finally taken from him, the furnaces near his palace burned for eight days. He "turn[ed] most of the Congo state records to ash and smoke."

He is reported to have said, "I will give them my Congo, but they have no right to know what I did there."

In the end, there was no rescue for the Congo. The Congo remains wrapped in war and destruction. Between 1998 and 2008 up to 5 million were killed in the Second Congo War.

It is a land blessed with tremendous natural wealth.

And it is a land that is constantly being harvested.

For the Congo, there has been no man in the desert.

The Menorah, which burns but is never consumed, represents another possibility. The Jewish people, who burn but are never consumed, represent another possibility. Ours is the path of creation and of life. Ours is the path of Hashem, who creates for six days and then rests – bringing timeless holiness to our world.

Ours is the path of harvesting, not to take from the future — but to give life and meaning to it.

Perhaps it is up to us - whomever we are - to be the bush burning in the desert. Perhaps it is up to us to give hope to our world.

Perhaps we can be that man in the desert, making whole that which has been destroyed.

A note on religion. The Congo was largely Christianized by this time. The use of minkasa *was actually a merging of native traditions with Christian connection to The Creator, called* Nzambi. *Modern Christian priests are often called* Nganga a Nzambi *or 'priests of God.'*

p.s. My mother's play, "Pharaoh, King of Egypt" formed the seed of my own exploration of the Torah. She passed away a few months after this story was written. The play can be found on YouTube.

Va'eira: The Contract

The thin material of the door thwacks weakly as I knock on it. I'm in the middle of a long hallway – made up of prefab building blocks linked together. The place looks decent, but the lines where the sections meet are marked by little bumps in the carpet and the walls. Nothing lines up quite perfectly.

The man who constructed this place, the man behind the door, cares far more about function than form.

"Come in," he says.

I push open the door and step into the office. The room is no more than 10 feet wide and 10 feet deep. Stuffed into it is a desk set against the back wall and two cheap swivel chairs.

The man in the room, Afsin Calari, pivots towards me and gestures with his hand. I sit in the other chair. There are bruises on Afsin's neck. I've never noticed them before.

"Close the door," he says. And I do.

I look at Afsin, waiting. I've known him for years and I still can't seem to understand what kind of a man he is.

"You did it," he announces, with a broad smile.

"Did what?" I ask.

"What I hired you for."

I look at him and tip my head, confused.

"The contract is renewed?" I ask.

"Yes." he says.

"How?"

Afsin smiles, turns to his computer and hits play on a video. I see it then, the video feed from another man's office. The clip is short.

The man behind the desk, a guy by the name of Mark Johnson, rises, runs across the room and wraps his hands around another man's neck. The violence and anger are extreme.

The man Mark Johnson is trying to kill is sitting right across from me.

The strange thing is, I can't blame Mark for what I see. Afsin, a man I had admired for so long, had behaved like a monster. I had helped him behave like a monster.

I just stare, my rage just barely checked, at the man in front of me.

Afsin sees my confusion. He sees my regret. And he smiles, again.

"Do you know why I picked you?"

I shake my head, no.

"Your brother came here when you were still a kid. You started visiting then. I remember when you first came, you were scared."

I don't remember that, but I can imagine it. Hundreds of high-functioning but developmentally challenged adults live here. I loved my brother, but entering this environment must have been overwhelming.

I nod.

"I think you felt bad," Afsin says, "That your parents sent your brother here."

"I was sad. And I was angry." That I remember.

"So, you visited him *all the time*. Your brother was visited more often than *anybody else* in this place. But you didn't just visit him. You began to visit everybody. I watched you change from a little boy who was scared of the people who live here to a man who was so full of love for all of them. You even began to understand *why* they lived here."

This is a lecture I've heard before. I decide to let Afsin speak. "They lived here because *I* believed that whenever possible, people should work. The vast majority of the people who live here work. Their lives are more fulfilling because of it. There are 472 adults living here who have meaning in their lives because of what we do."

I nod again, I know all of this.

Afsin continues, "But it isn't easy finding them jobs. Which is why the airport contract is so important. There are 472 adults here. And they all have jobs. They clean out garbage bins, they sweep floors, they mop bathrooms, they hold signs, some even do simple inventory. They all have jobs, meaningful jobs. And in a way, they are the face of our city."

I nod.

"But then their jobs were threatened. Mark Johnson controlled the contract at the airport, and he was threatening to cancel it."

"I know all this," I say, just barely keeping my cool.

Afsin continues as if I hadn't spoken. "So, I hired you. I picked you because people love you. Because people open up to you. And I needed Mark to open up to you."

"You hired me to become his friend. And then you used me to destroy him."

"No, you saved him. We saved him."

"How?" I demand.

"You became his friend. His real friend. You found him drinking at a bar and you talked to him. He needed a friend, and you became his friend."

"I was no friend," I say, "I just dug up dirt on him and then you showed up in his office, again and again, and you hurled insults at him. I'd find out his wife left him because she thought he was a nobody. And you'd go to his office and tell him no woman would want him because he was a nobody. And then I'd find out he once wanted to run his own business and you went and told him he lacked the guts to do it. I found out his parents liked his older brother more and you somehow used *that* to insult him. Everything, constantly, was beating him down. You used what he shared with me to destroy him."

Afsin just smiles.

I just want to punch him. I felt horrible. I love people. "I loved Mark and you used that to destroy him."

"So why didn't you stop?"

"I was ashamed. Once I worked out what you were doing, I was too ashamed to admit my part."

"Good."

"Good?!?" I demand. "He told me what you said, every time. He told me how you humiliated him. I saw the man cry and steam. He was ready to burst."

"Yes," says Afsin, plainly.

"*We* tortured him for months. Don't you normally kiss up to somebody when you want to renew a contract?"

Afsin steeples his fingers and looks at me carefully.

After a long pause, he speaks, "Do you know *how* I learned that he wanted to cancel our deal?"

"No," I say.

"Our price was competitive. Our people work slowly, but there are government grants that help make up the difference. I even donate a fair amount of money myself."

I could believe it. Despite the cheap digs, Afsin has the air of tremendous wealth.

"So, what was the problem?"

"Mark told us he'd been receiving feedback from travelers. They said they were uncomfortable around our people. Just like you were when you were a child."

"I could believe it," I say.

"I could too," says Afsin, "But I wanted to understand it better. Maybe I could do something to help. Maybe one particular position was the problem. So, I had a friend recover the records. Do you know what I found?"

"No," I say.

"The forms filled out by hand were filled out in Mark's handwriting. He tried to conceal it by changing his script here and there. But they were all in his handwriting. And the forms filled out online all traced back to a single library IP address. The library closest to his house."

"What does that mean?" I ask.

"It means that Mark *created* the passengers who complained about our people."

"But why would he do that?"

"Mark was a weak man," Afsin says, "He wanted to *matter*, desperately. He wanted recognition. He wanted to be important in the ways people measure. He wanted pride. When a more *colorful* service provider came to him, he was ready to listen. There was only one problem, they wanted to charge more than we did."

"So, they wouldn't win the contract," I say.

"But they could win the contract. They really wanted it. They could rent out over 400 people and get $10 an hour doing it. That's

$32,000 a day and $10 million a year. So, they paid Mark Johnson a *bribe*."

"What?!?" I splutter.

"A friend of mine reviewed his bank accounts. He took a bribe."

"Are you sure?"

"Of course."

"So why didn't you just report him?"

"Because I respect him," says Afsin.

"So, you insulted him instead?"

"Mark wanted to matter. He wanted to start his own business. He wanted to be proud. He wanted a wife who wanted him. But he had to be proud for a reason, not because he had a few hundred thousand illicit dollars in his bank account. That would just eat at his pride."

"The solution was to insult him?"

"The solution was to hire you to be his friend. You learned about him. And I used what *you* learned to drive him crazy. Do you know what I said the last time?"

"I don't," I say.

"You told me his son got straight Cs on a report card. You told me the kid didn't care. I went to Mark, in his office, and told him we'd save the child a space – in our facility."

I want to just whistle. I love the people who live here, but I can see a man finding a deep insult in what Afsin had said.

"No wonder he attacked you."

"I deserved it," Afsin says with a smile, "But it worked out. He got fired and we got our contract back."

"But you destroyed him to do it?"

"Do you really care about a man who took a bribe that could have hurt hundreds of vulnerable people?"

I think about it, but only for a moment. "I do, yes," I say.

Afsin answers even more quickly, "Good. So, think about what *we* did. He got fired for attacking me and I won't press charges. Do you know what that means?"

"No..." I say.

"He *didn't* get fired for taking a bribe. He *didn't* go to prison. He got fired protecting his *honor*, not losing it. It was a kindness."

"What does he do next?"

"He stood up for himself. He stood up to me. And he took a risk."

"He did..."

Afsin continues, "He's taking the first step in defending his honor. So now he can earn it. He might find a woman who respects him. He might find that his son can begin to care. Perhaps he could even start a business."

"With what money? I'm sure the 'colorful' folk will take back their donation."

"Well, he has a friend. You could help him. And behind the scenes, I could lend you the money to help get him started."

I look at Afsin then. And for the first time, I see him. Once I saw what he was doing with my brother, I thought he was a saint. But when he was using me to destroy Mark, I thought he was a demon. Now I know he is complex, complex but somehow wonderful.

In the end, because of him, everybody won. Everybody but the 'colorful' contractors.

Somehow, everybody won.

Stop for a moment and pretend the story of the Exodus ended as this week's Torah reading does: with the plague of hail. Pretend we don't know the conclusion.

If you stop here, you can describe Moshe in one word: 'reluctant'. Moshe doesn't want to carry out the mission Hashem chooses for him. He resists. Then he delays. Even when he finally comes to Egypt there are issues. When he first speaks before the people, they fail to listen because of Ketzer Ruach – shortness of spirit. Perhaps Moshe is the one who lacks conviction. Perhaps that is *why* they fail to listen.

Then he complains of uncircumcised lips. In ancient Egypt, a prophet would speak the words of the god they were representing, without a filter. When Moshe complains that he has uncircumcised lips, he is saying that he cannot speak with conviction. His channeling of the divine is impeded.

The people will not listen to him, and so, neither will Pharaoh.

It continues with the plagues; Moshe begs Pharaoh not to resist. And he prays again and again for Hashem to lift the plagues themselves. Moshe sees massive destruction; he does not see liberation. He is in the dark about Hashem's greater plan. He *needs* to resist G-d's actions so that the thrust of the story is not the glee of destruction but the power of Pharaoh's pride.

Moshe is just like the man in this story. He loves Egypt and the royal family he grew up with, despite their sins. He can't see the greater picture. If he had seen that picture, he would be unable to play his part; begging Pharaoh to relent in the vain hope of protecting him, Left in the dark, Moshe struggles to reconcile the wonder of Hashem with the destruction Hashem is unleashing.

Years ago, my mother wrote a play "Pharaoh, King of Egypt." It explored the story of the Exodus from the Egyptian side. Pharaoh was made the most powerful of men so that he could become an object lesson in the limits of human pride. Her play focused on Pharaoh's pride and his need to defend it at all costs. Knowing the presence of G-d only strengthens his resolve.

In the end, Pharaoh is destroyed in every practical sense. But in the end, he somehow keeps his honor. Perhaps Pharaoh shares that with Mark Johnson.

Perhaps both were redeemed by their struggles.

Bo: The Haversham Trust

The view out the windshield of the car is dark and shifting. There's no rain. My headlights pick up the shape of the uneven pavement as they bounce over it. My window is open, warm air rushing into the cabin of the truck – keeping me alert and awake. The air smells of evergreen forests and dirt. I weave slightly on the road, crossing the median here and there. But nobody minds. There's no traffic and the median is more of a recommendation than a reality.

I know I'll be home soon.

Then, out of nowhere, there's a dark figure. A shape. I look towards it, curious, and the truck seems to follow my eyes. The lights illuminate a face just as it turns towards me. My foot reaches for the brake. But it is far too slow. I feel it then, through the steering wheel and the floor of the truck. Everything else was so indistinct. But not that. I feel every bone that breaks as the front of the truck connects with the surprised face before me.

I scream.

When I open my eyes, I am where I always am.

The sofa I'm on is old. It has cloth fabric that smells vaguely of rot. There's a beer in my hand. And in front of me, the TV is playing. It is a rebroadcast of a classic football game. I know every down and throw by heart. I feel like I've seen it a million times. The volume is up, loud. I can hear, almost feel, the crunch of bones with the most brutal of the tackles.

I'd fallen asleep, that was all.

The game had led to the nightmare.

34

I look at the beer in my hand. I curse it. And then in one long series of swallows, I finish it off.

I turn off the TV. I look around my dark little house, with its stained walls, low ceiling and cozy, molding, smell. It seems so small. And yet it feels so empty. I think about getting up. Brushing my teeth. Going to bed. But I don't feel up to it. Instead, I drop the beer on the floor – alongside a few others – and then I tip my head back on the sofa and fall fast asleep.

I wake up in the morning a little late, as I always do. I rush here and there, showering and brushing my teeth so it isn't completely obvious how I've spent my night. And then I race out to my truck, start it up and head into town. I've got a job. I'm a cashier at the local supermarket. It's an 8-to-5 gig with a healthy lunch break. Union rules. And the people are nice enough, even if they aren't the most ambitious of folk.

I'd wanted more, once. I'd had more. I'd been a football player in high school. I'd thought I was pretty good. I was the star of the school, and I was the quarterback. I thought I'd go to college, and maybe – if things broke just right – the NFL. But no colleges called. My girlfriend, her name was Amy, was just as disappointed as I was. I was her ticket up and out. She didn't leave me, though. I was proud of that, of us.

I was proud our relationship could survive that kind of hit.

I did go to college, just not some fancy four-year place. Instead, I got a degree at a local community college. I was licensed as a CNA, a Certified Nursing Assistant. The money wasn't much, but I felt like I was helping. And Amy was proud of me. We got married. We even bought a little house near town, up a little hill from the heart of the place. Things were pretty good. Before long, we had two children. A little boy and a little girl.

The problem was that Amy had moved on from my college dreams, but I hadn't. Not really. I'd still wanted the glory football could offer. I'd wanted those games, that attention, those titles. I knew I could never have them, though. It wasn't why I'd started drinking – being a star high-school quarterback will get you started – but it was why the drinking began to take over my life.

I'd get home every day. And I'd pop open a beer, or two, or six. I hated myself for it. I should be doing more. I should be spending my life in some sort of useful way. I promised myself I would, eventually. Right after the next beer or two. After all, I'd worked hard that day. I deserved a little break.

Amy used to scream at me then, even in front of the kids.

"You shouldn't drink like that," she'd shout. "You're settin' a bad example for the kids."

I could have ignored her. But I didn't. She was right. I needed to do more with myself. Somehow, I could. I'd looked up degree programs then, to become a Registered Nurse or some such. But I never did anything about it. Maybe I was afraid of failing a second time.

What I did instead was start drinking outside of the house. Occasional visits to the bar with my buddies turned into nightly affairs. When my parents passed, one after another in one short year, Amy tried to comfort me. But I didn't seek *her* out. Instead, I just drank more. I'd stumble out of the bar to my truck and drive just a few short miles to my house. When I'd eventually slip into bed, Amy would ignore me. She'd given up on me. At least that's what I remembered. I had already started to suffer the blackouts.

When I'd wake up in the morning, I'd start it all over again.

That was when the nightmares started.

Not long after, Amy left.

It was so simple. One day, when I got home, she just wasn't there. She didn't leave a note. She didn't need to.

I knew why she was gone.

I thought about stopping then. Maybe I could get her back.

"I'd do it!" I decided. But I needed a beer first. You know, to fortify myself for the effort.

I never did stop. I just got worse and worse. I'd be late to work. And the empty house began to fall apart around me. It wasn't long before I lost my job as a CNA. I just barely managed to get another at the supermarket.

Even that wasn't enough. I couldn't seem to dig myself a deep enough hole. Eventually, I told myself, I'd hit bottom. Then, finally, I'd have what it took to get back up and make something of myself. But my definition of bottom just kept shifting further and further away.

That's where I am now. I sit on the couch, watching the TV. Hating myself. I go to sleep, wake up, and repeat. Things get worse. My boss at the supermarket threatens me with termination. I don't particularly care, though. I deserve termination. I lack the will to resist it.

One morning, on my way to work, I notice a billboard that's gone up on my little road into town. It is a huge thing, and it is advertising something called "The Haversham Trust." There is a picture of a smiling man wearing hospital scrubs and carrying some sort of tablet computer. I have no idea what a "Haversham Trust" is. But I don't really care. People can advertise whatever they want to. It's a free country. The odd thing about the sign is where it is. It is on my little road, not the main highway. Maybe a hundred people a day drive past it, instead of the thousands who would see it on the main drag. It is like somebody had sold the Haversham Trust a pricey billboard that is really worth next to nothing.

Then again, it is a free country.

I drive by the sign every day, on my way to work. And once in a while I see it in my rearview mirror as I drive by it at night on my way home from the bar. I ignore it, every day. And then the Haversham Trust doubles down. They buy another billboard, in the same spot, facing the other direction. I can't help but see it then, every day and every night. The same smiling man with the same little tablet computer.

One night, I'm heading up my road when the headlight from my truck (the one that works) flashes over the sign. This time, I just stop the truck. Right there below that sign. I don't know why. I look up at the sign, and I finally read it. "Haversham Trust" it says. Underneath, in a smooth cursive text, it reads "Reinvent yourself through Industry and Charity."

I'm pretty drunk, as I normally am. But the guy on the poster kind of looks like me; or would if I lost twenty pounds, shaved and got a decent haircut. There is a web address at the bottom of the poster. I get out my phone, punch it in, and see an address. The Haversham Trust has an office, in the town. It is in a tiny rundown strip mall right across the road from my favorite bar.

Why would somebody who has an office in this town buy a sign on my road? Why would they buy two?

I decide I am going to ask them. I stick the truck into gear, pull a U-turn across the 'advisory' medium, and head back into town. The Trust is closed when I get there. But it isn't such a cold night. So, I kill the engine and just park. I have a six-pack on the seat next to me. I think about cracking one open. But I'm suddenly aware one beer won't do much for me and I don't feel up to drinking six.

Instead, I recline my seat, and I go to sleep right there. I'll see what the Haversham Trust is in the morning.

I wake up with the sun shining through the windshield. I feel awful, but that is par for the course. I think about heading up to the house, getting a shower, freshening up. I don't do it, though. I just want to ask the Trust a question. So, I bring my seat up, open the squeaking door of my truck and step out into the morning light. I look at my phone. It is 9AM. I am way too late to show up at work.

The Trust is open, though. I walk up to it and pull the glass door. One of those bell things announces my arrival, but it is deeper and more mellifluous than any bell I've ever heard before. I step inside. I expect linoleum floors, or some cheap industrial carpeting. I expect a little Formica counter. I expect some cheap furniture and maybe a pimple-nosed attendant. But that's not what I see.

Instead, as I step into the room, my feet seem to melt into an exquisite Persian carpet. The edges of the room are lined with ornate bookshelves in some dark wood. Expensive-looking scones of light hang on the walls. The place feels... holy. I feel suddenly, totally, dirty. I lean down and unlace my shoes. I step out of them carefully and set them to the side of the door.

And then I pad further into the magnificent little storefront.

In the middle of the room, there is a desk. It is angled up a bit, like an architect's desk. There is a lip at the bottom, to hold books up.

39

The desk seems huge, but it is only four feet on a side. The impression of size comes from its design. It is a solid wood affair, with complex and beautiful carvings.

A matching chair sits before it. It is empty.

"Hello?" I say, calling out for help. But nobody replies. There seems to be nobody here.

I step up to the bookshelves and I begin to look at the titles. They are all stories; there is not a textbook to be seen. I take down one of the books, I carry it to the desk, and I start reading. I spend the entire day there, reading. I read the stories; stories of men and women who overcame themselves. Stories of people who overcame their own faults. They are old stories, all of them. Some seem set hundreds of years in the past. Nonetheless, they all seem to be speaking just to me. I spend the whole day there, by myself. When the lights dim in the evening, I realize the place is closing.

I get up, go to the door, step into my shoes and drive home, sober.

And then I come back, first thing in the morning. The place is open, but I've seen nobody open it.

A few days later, I lose my job. I get a notice in the mail. But it doesn't seem to matter. I have a new addiction. I am reading those books and falling into those stories. My house is foreclosed on soon afterwards. But I still have my truck. I park it there, outside the Haversham Trust. There is an old bathroom in the strip mall. Between that, my truck, a nearby supermarket and the Trust, I seem to have everything I need. At least until my meager cash runs out.

Then I realize that the stories are more than just stories. They are guidebooks for my own life. I can conquer myself, my own limits, through industry and charity.

These people can serve as my example.

I apply for another job then, as a CNA. There is only one hospital in town, and they don't want to hire me back. I look like crap, but I'm not drunk and they're desperate for staff. That first day, I use the employee locker room to clean up. I spend a part of my first paycheck on a haircut and shave. I don't drive to work though. I walk to and from that little strip mall. I don't want to spend the money on gas.

Instead, for the first time in my life, I am truly saving money.

Not that I deserve any of it.

This time in the hospital is different than the last. When it comes to the patients, I'm not a doctor or even a nurse. I'm just a body helping them out. But they love to talk, and they deserve somebody who can listen. Soon, patients begin to ask for me by name. It doesn't matter who they are. High flyin' types or the parents of my old buddies from the bar. They are asking for me because they love me, and I love them. They are in pain, life-threatening pain. I am in pain too, not physical pain, but something threatens my existence, nonetheless.

I park in front of the Trust every night. It is across the street from my old bar. I want to go into that bar. Not because I want a drink, but because I want to destroy myself. Despite everything I do at the hospital, I feel like self-destruction is all I have earned. I can't explain it, but I know it is true.

The only thing that keeps me going are those stories. I read and reread them. They tell me, no matter what the voices in my own head say, that I can recover. That I too can conquer my demons. That I can be *worthy* of success. They begin to fill me, those stories. And I begin to plot my own story. I *will* become a Registered Nurse, like the guy on the billboard. Perhaps I'll become a Nurse Practitioner. Patients will rely on me, and I will be there for them in their darkest times.

I will be a light for them.

I can almost taste that reality. But I *know* I do not deserve it.

I just can't understand why.

Then, one night, I fall asleep in the Trust. My head comes down on the table. And the old nightmare returns. I feel the crunch of bones as they're driven into the front of my truck. And I awake with a scream. It all seems so incredibly real.

Then, with a sickening thought, I realize that it might be.

I'd been suffering blackouts.

I could have killed someone.

I pull out my phone and I search the news. I must have had that dream, for the first time, three years ago. It must have been summer; the wind was warm.

It doesn't take long to find. The town isn't that big. That summer, three years earlier, a fourteen-year-old boy had been killed in a hit-and-run. His name had been John Olsen.

The driver was never found.

I just stare at the page. My heart drops out of me. Almost in shock, I stand up on shaking legs and head for the door. I stumble out of the Trust, forgetting to put on my shoes or my coat. It is raining. In my bare feet, I kneel in front of the truck, and I look closely at the broken light.

And then I see it.

A fracture in the plastic. A hairline crack that tells me I killed a child.

I know then that I deserve whatever fate I suffer.

I don't know how long I sit there, the cold rain coming down on me. I consider crossing the street. I consider having a beer and then another and then drinking myself to death. I consider going to the police and turning myself in. Then I consider the family. I look on the phone again. I read the name again. And I realize I know it.

The father's name is Mark Olsen.

I know him from the hospital. He's a hollow shell of man who suffered a heart attack at 43.

His son was killed three years earlier.

I begin to walk then. Towards the man's house, towards where I used to live. I just walk, not even putting on my shoes. It is cold, dark and wet. But I deserve the pain. I deserve the risk.

It must be close to midnight when I show up at the man's door. I ring the bell and a few minutes later a worn-down man, Mark Olsen, answers the door. He sees me. He knows me. He invites me in.

I sit in his kitchen, still shaking. He offers me tea. His wife comes in, she's wearing a night robe. She also knows me. She also offers me tea. They love me in their way.

But I turn them down. I turn them both down.

This is an empty shell of a house. He is an empty shell of a man. And she of a woman.

And I caused all of it.

I look at them then, shaking uncontrollably. I want to tell the whole story. I want to share the reasons I drank. But no reason can justify what I did. All I can do is offer myself and my future to them.

As calmly as I can manage, I say, "I didn't know it until just now. But I killed your son."

The faces look at me, uncomprehending. And then I tell them my nightmare. I tell them what I can remember. I tell them about the truck. I tell them that I surrender myself to them completely. They will decide my fate.

I expect rage, but there is only kindness.

The woman makes a pot of tea. She pours me a cup.

The man adds a bit of milk and a bit of sugar.

It is my turn to not understand.

"We know you, now" the man says.

I nod, uncomprehending.

"And we admire you," the woman adds.

I just stare at them.

And then the man says, "If you were the man who killed our son, you would not leave this house. But you are no longer that man. And so, we pray that you can live the life our son couldn't."

I sit there for what seems like forever. I drink their tea. And I listen to stories of their only child. I listen to the dreams they had for him. They prayed that he would have a life of industry and charity.

I know that his dreams must become mine.

In the morning, they loan me a coat and shoes and I walk, as I always do, to work.

I walk past where the billboards used to be, but somebody has taken them down.

It doesn't surprise me; I haven't been on this road in months.

At the end of the day, I walk back to the little strip mall. As I always do.

My truck is there, parked where it always is. But the Haversham Trust is nowhere to be seen. There is nothing but an empty storefront in a rundown mall. Dust floats through that store, coating every available surface. Like it has been collecting there for years.

I just stand in front of the window, looking at the emptiness.

And then I know what I must do.

I must write my own story.

Perhaps, in time, it can find a way to inspire others.

The final plague that strikes the Egyptians is the Death of the First Born. The other plagues show G-d's power in three dimensions – rising from the river below to the sky above and then encompassing all with the darkness. But the Death of the First Born adds a fourth dimension. Time. G-d claims the future when he takes the first-born of Egypt. But He does not take the first-born of Israel. Instead, the Jewish people bring a Pascal Offering. By putting the blood of the offering on the door post, they somehow protect against this plague. Just as blood defines an organism, this blood defines a people. Each household is a cell, somehow brought together as a nation in service of Hashem.

The obvious question is how does the Pesach Offering protect us from the plague? The answer lays in the word used for the animal to be offered. It is called a *se*. The first time the word is used, it is used in the context of the sacrifice of Yitzchak by Avraham. Yitzchak asks where the *se* is and Avraham tells him that G-d will provide one. Yitzchak is the first *se*. Yitzchak is Avraham's future. The *se* represents *our* future. The Pesach Offering is a symbolic recreation of the Akeidah.

With the Pesach *Se*, we offer our future to Hashem. That sacrifice defines us, protects us and frees us.

Of course, this symbolism is not based on a single word alone. Every aspect of this offering reinforces the concept. The *se* is young because it represents the future. The *se* is male because it represents

45

the positive will to reproduce – and thus continue into the future. And the *se* is burnt, just like Yitzchak was supposed to be, because burning is how offerings are sent to Hashem. The *se* itself is chosen because both sheep and goats are meandering animals – they represent the Jewish people.

When we bring the *se* into our homes, we make it a part of the family. And whether through fire or eating, every part of the *se* is consumed. Just as Avraham trusted that Hashem would provide *his* future, we trust that Hashem will provide ours. We preserve nothing for contingencies. The eating is done with the people ready to move in order to reinforce this. Even though nothing has happened, they are showing their trust that something *will happen*. They are showing their trust in Hashem.

The timing strengthens it further. There are ten days without the *se*. These days represent the ten plagues. On the tenth day, the future is taken from the Egyptians and the future – through emancipation – is given to the Jewish people. This is the day we bring the *se* into our homes. Then there are four days where the people have a future, as represented by the *se*. This correlates to the four major miracles in the desert before the giving of the Torah. Finally, on the eve of the fifteenth miracle – the giving of the Torah – the people dedicate their future to G-d by saying 'all G-d has spoken, we will do'. Just as with the Akeidah, they agree to that which they do not understand.

That fifteenth day is represented by the Pesach Offering itself.

The Pesach Offering is a sacrifice of complete surrender by a people who had no power.

The man in the story puts his future entirely in the hands of the Hansens; and is granted a future because of that gift.

We do the same. Hashem grants us a future – as his people – *because* we offer our future to Him.

The man in the story sacrifices himself to a couple who only want to raise him up. Likewise, we sacrifice ourselves to Hashem –who wants only to raise us up so that we can serve our ultimate purpose: represent His values in the world.

Not coincidentally, those values are the same as the values learned by the man in the story.

They are the values of Creation and Rest.

They are the values of Industry and Charity.

Beshalach: Busan

My chair is pushed back just a bit from the table in front of me. A low light hangs over it, piercing the cloud of cigarette smoke and illuminating the rough and desperate faces that surround it. Waitresses circulate, wearing clothes too close cut to be appropriate in any normal establishment. Of course, this place is not proper or established or appropriate. Just being here breaks the law. But it is where I am.

It is where I have fallen to. No other casinos will allow me to play.

I order another Soju and look at the cards in my hand. It is not a good hand. But perhaps there is a chance I will win. I pull back the clear liquid in a single gulp and then lay 10 portraits of Shin Saimdang, the great woman artist of 500-years past, on the table. Each portrait graces the front of a 50,000 won note. It is 500,000 won. 500,000 won I have *just* borrowed from the house.

My debt is almost 50 million.

I watch as the dealer deals his cards, and my fate is written for me. I cannot win this hand. As I watch, passively, the players circle. They fold, one after another. But one does not. I look at him, praying that he too will fold. He is a tough man, but old. He must be in his seventies. His face is rough and worn. He's wearing glasses and gaudy, but tired-looking, clothes. He grimaces, and all his features seem to fall into the entirely of the motion. I realize I'm staring, desperately. He glances at me. His eyes are hard, and I am afraid he will see my weakness, or take umbrage at my stare.

I look quickly away, and down at the table.

I know my place. I must respect it.

48

My heart drops as he lays down his cards.

He has not folded. I do not know what I can possibly do.

At that moment, the dealer asks, "Would you like to extend your loan?"

I want to say yes. I want to stay in the game. I want a chance. How much worse can it get? The dealer is about to press his offer, perhaps specify it in more detail. But then the man in the gaudy outfit makes a small motion with his hand and the dealer falls suddenly silent.

I understand then.

The casino belongs to him.

The man in the gaudy outfit looks at me. Then he stands slowly and gestures with his hand, as if he is inviting me towards him. I know who he is now. He is a *jopok,* a gangster. He will be the one to collect my debt.

As if on a string, I begin to circle the table towards him. A million thoughts run through my mind. Perhaps my stare insulted him. Perhaps I have damaged his *kibun*; his 'face', his 'presence' before the others here. Perhaps this is the end of me.

But then I realize that is not how they think. They want money, all of them. Perhaps he simply believes I could never pay off a debt greater than the one I have now. Perhaps, now, he will tell me what I must do to make him whole. There's a chance I could survive.

As I come towards him, the *jopok* wraps his hand around my shoulder. I want to shake off the unwelcome touch. We do not know each other. We are not friends. It is not appropriate. But I am small, and he is not. Or at least he does not think he is. I bow my head and allow myself to be guided to a table in a corner of the room.

I stay calm, but inside I am shaking with a strange combination of insult and fear.

49

The man holds up his hand and a scantily clad waitress comes over. Unlike the others, she is not Korean. She is tall and blond. She seems European. She does not come to take an order, though. She comes with a bottle of Soju, glasses, some snacks and a slip of paper. She already knows what the old man wants.

She puts a bottle and two small glasses on the table. Then she lays the paper on the table, face down in front of the old man.

The old man then leans forward and pours me a drink, as if he is my host. I reach forward and do the same for him, trying to keep my hands from shaking.

We sit then, across from one another, the glasses in front of us. I'm staring at the table, but I can feel the man's eyes boring into me.

"It would be rude not to drink," he says, suddenly. My arm shoots forward then and I grasp the glass. I lift it almost robotically and our glasses touch.

"Konbe" we pronounce, together and then both of us drink.

He pours another for me, and I pour another for him. Then we sit, silently.

After what seems like an eternity, he asks, "Do you have a family?"

I lift up my eyes and look at him briefly, confused. Is he threatening my family?

He continues, "This is not business, not yet. Just a question. Do you have a family?"

"No," I answer, cautiously.

He nods and we lapse back into silence.

A minute later, he speaks again. "Where did you get your mathematics training?"

My eyes shoot up. Is my debt so large that he has researched me so carefully?

"Kim Il Sung University," I say.

"Ahhh," he answers, pursing his lips. We sit then, silently. He rolls his drink in his glass. I wait.

"Do you know how long I've been a *jopok*?" he asks.

I shake my head, no.

"Almost 60 years now, can you believe that?"

I shake my head, yes. It can never hurt to agree with a man like him.

"When I got started, it was an honorable thing; almost. In those days, in the late 1950s, the Japanese Yakuza dominated so much of our economy. They owned government ministers, and they directed the activities of so many of our businesses. Our legal system was corrupt and so we had to fight back, outside the law."

The old man reaches towards a small bowl of flavored nuts. The smell of sugar, fish-sauce, garlic and chili sparks into the air as he bites into the first of the nuts.

Then he continues, "Our gang was poor. They all were. We were there to push out the Japanese, and everything we had was poured into that. We forced others, businessmen, to fund us. We ran protection rings and prostitution rings and numbers rackets. But we were building Korea. I felt proud then, of what I was doing."

The man slowly unbuttoned the top of his shirt. He pulls it open, revealing not only leathered skin but also a tattoo of twin dragons.

"You see this," he says, nodding his head towards his chest, "I used to walk around with my shirt open. People could know I was a gangster. But then... things changed. The government became stronger, and they managed to crack down on the gangs. All the

51

gangs. Most of us left this life. A tattoo like this could land you in jail. I covered it then. I hid who I was. But I was a gangster, and I stayed a gangster. For decades, I remained a gangster."

"What service do you do now?" I ask.

The old man smiles. "Every society, even ours, has those who are stupid or irresponsible. They can cause immense damage and chaos. But few people are willing to step in and control them. When they come to me, to play cards or to borrow money for foolish ventures, I enable them to do so. But when it comes time to collect, I don't threaten them with death. That's not how Korea works. I would be erased if I killed a man over a debt. No, I just threaten the harmony of their families. I threaten them with embarrassment. The families pay up, their wayward sons become... more cautious. The families make them act appropriately. Bruises caused by one of my men, bruises seen by others, would be a disgrace too great to bear."

He takes another handful of nuts and slowly places one in his mouth. He chews slowly. I hear each crunch of his teeth.

"I am not a skilled man," he says, at last, "But you are. You have mathematics."

I nod.

"And you fled North Korea."

I nod again. My accent, my clothes and my mannerisms tend to give it away. North Koreans are far more conservative than even their highly conservative southern counterparts.

The man continues, "Many North Koreans come here, to my casinos. But it is generally because they are both stupid and irresponsible. They are country bumpkins who do not really understand the games and who never learned to be responsible. They think they can just *win* money. They do not work with others to make real things. They don't have 'others'."

"But they often do not have families," I say, "How do you collect from them?"

I'm wondering what the man has in store for me.

"It is not so hard," the man says, "I force them to buy fake investments with the money they owe me. The investments collapse, then I take their money. Their stipends are transferred directly to my accounts and the courts enforce my judgments. Nobody really comes to help them. They are an embarrassment."

I lower my eyes again. I'd expected as much. Perhaps that slip of paper is a contract.

"But you are different," the man says, "I've watched you play. They play to win, because on some level or another they don't understand that they can't really win. But you play *in order to lose*."

"What?" I ask, surprised.

"You always know," the old man says, "When you have a good hand, or not. When you have a strong hand, you bid like it is weak. When you have a weak one... you bid like it is strong. You play to lose. That intrigues me."

He smiles for a moment. Then he asks, "So why are you in my club, losing at poker?"

I can't really answer him. I don't know what to say. I didn't know I was playing to lose.

"Let me ask another way," the man says, "Why did you, a mathematician, leave the North?"

I feel my face burning.

"Shame," the man says, "Tell me about your shame."

"I was a loyal patriot," I say, "My parents were patriots, sent abroad to serve the State. I don't know what they do... or did. But I was taken in by the State. I was raised by the State. The State realized that I was a talented mathematician. I won a place at Kim Il Sung University. I studied statistics. And then I got a job at the Central Statistics Bureau."

"In Pyongyang?" the old man asks.

"Yes," I say, "I was in the Central Office. Most of our work was never meant to be published. We only shared a little information about population and electricity use. Because our enemies could see what we published, that information was fabricated. Our real purpose was to guide the State. So, we tracked all kinds of information – even the loyalty of different cities and provinces. I was good at my job. Very good. I rose quickly through the ranks and before long I was reporting to the Director General himself."

"Impressive," says the old man.

"I was proud," I say. "Up until that point, I had had routine work. I had prepared numerous reports. But those reports stayed within the Bureau. In my new position, I was to review the work of others. I was to collect and summarize what they had done so that it could be passed on. Perhaps even to the Dear Respected Comrade, Kim Jon Un himself."

"So, what went wrong?" the old man says.

"The first month, I did exactly as I was told. I took my first reports, and I cleaned them up and I summarized them. I proudly presented my work before the assembled heads of many agencies. The Director General was there, as was the senior leadership of the Agricultural Bureau, the Industrial Bureau, the Propaganda Bureau and so many others."

"And?"

"As I spoke, the Director General's face grew darker and darker. I didn't know what I was doing wrong, but his anger boiled up within him. I grew less and less certain. I had thought my work was strong. Then, in front of everybody, he said I was an imbecile and an idiot. I lowered my eyes and I listened. But I didn't really understand. I had done my work properly. I was a patriot. Then the Director General continued. He stated new results, new outcomes. New facts. They were better and stronger than what I had shared. I didn't understand where they had come from. Then, bit by bit, I did. The lower levels of the Bureau collected data on our *reality*, perhaps. But the highest levels of government never saw *that* information. My job was to create a believable *new* reality, one that fit with prior reports and one that could be carried into the future. I was there to craft a reality that made them all look good, and believable, in front of the Dear Respected Comrade."

"What happened next?"

"The Director General asked if I agreed with his conclusions. I said he was completely right. I apologized for my stupidity. I was afraid I would lose my job – or worse. But I didn't. They had brought me there to destroy my *kibun*. I had to be broken so I would understand what was really expected of me. I learned. But I never recovered. I had believed in the State, in the Dear Respected Comrade. But now I knew we were all weaving lies. We were all puppets on the strings of men like the Director General."

"So, you left?"

"Not right away. It took years before I had a chance. I just did what they told me, and I did it well. The State found me a suitable woman. But we never really connected. Thankfully, we never had a child. Then, five years later, I was sent on a survey of a northern border region. It was along the Yalu River, but not in a major city. I lied to a guard and told him I was there to inspect a bridge across the river. He wanted to check, but I was from Pyongyang and I reported to a Director General. And so, he let me inspect the bridge. I walked most of the way across, got underneath 'inspecting the girders' and then slipped into the water and crossed in China. I thought I was free."

"Of course," the old man says, "You weren't."

"No," I say, "I wasn't. Other North Koreans, many of them, had fled into China. The Chinese government pursued them and sent them back. If they were caught, they were likely to die. They and their families alike. All of us were running and hiding. We were living in an authoritarian country with the best tracking systems in the world and we were trying, as hard as we could, to escape. I spent years there, always afraid of being captured. I knew a great deal more than most refugees and so I knew I was a valuable target. I ate fatty foods to bulk up my face and I cut my own cheek to confuse the facial recognition systems. Eventually, I made it to Thailand and the South Korean embassy there."

"And you came here?"

"I came here. When I got off the airplane, I felt such relief and such joy. I was no longer a puppet. I was no longer locked into a single path – of service or of flight. I was breathing the free air of Korea. That was two months ago."

"And already," the old man says, "You have come to me."

I nod.

The old man asks, "Why?"

"Why what?"

56

"Why are you here, in my casino?"

I look at him then.

"I don't know," I say.

"Are you frightened?" he asks.

"Of you?"

"No," he says, "Are you frightened, in general?"

I think about it. Then I realize that I am. I am more frightened than I ever have been before. I don't even have to speak; the man sees it on my face.

"What of?" he asks.

"I, I don't know." I say.

"Is it starvation?" he asks.

I shake my head, no.

"Imprisonment?"

No.

"Shame?"

I find myself nodding. Yes. Yes. I live in fear of shame. It is the greatest fear I have ever had.

The old man smiles then. "You are a smart man. An educated man. An accomplished man. A driven man. And now a free man."

I nod.

"That is why you are frightened."

"I don't understand," I say.

"You have the fear of all great free men: you are afraid of not living up to your potential."

I think about it. And then I know it is true.

"In the North," the old man says, "You could not make your own choices. If things went poorly, it was not your fault. But here, if you fail, there is no such excuse."

I nod.

"So, let me ask you again. Why are you here in my casino? Why are you playing to lose?"

"I don't know," I laugh nervously, shame beginning to run through me.

"But I do," says the man, "You are trying to escape. You are trying to destroy yourself so you don't have to feel the shame of *trying* to succeed – and perhaps failing along the way."

I sit there. My drink in my hand. And I know the old man is right.

He smiles again. "You are a mathematician," he says, "A statistician. If you lose a hand, does it mean you should not have bet on it?"

"No," I say.

"Correct," says the man, "You play the odds. If you play them well, you will lose some hands that are strong and win some that are weak. But you play the odds. You can't regret placing a bet when the statistics told you it was the right thing to do."

I nod. He is right, of course.

"A good hand is still good even if it doesn't win and a bad hand is still bad even if it does."

I nod, again.

The old man continues, "This is how you can survive your freedom. You must make the right choices, not because you know the future. But because they are the right choices. They are at one with *inhwa*, with harmonious living. Then you live with the consequences. You may acquire *kibun* in the eyes of others. You may acquire flashy cars and nice houses and a good family. You already have education. Or you may not. But you *will* acquire kibun in your own eyes, and you *will* find joy in your decisions you make."

58

We sit there again, in the silence. I think about what the man has said. And then I ask him, "Have you found joy in your decisions?"

The old man smiles again. I see a tired bitterness in it. "No," he says, "I have made the wrong choices. I sought the empty pride of a *jopok* when a *jopok* was needed. I put the ends before the means. I can lie to myself, but I know I have not acted for harmony, for *inhwa*. I hide my tattoos in shame. I rarely get a chance to taste the sweetness of my own freedom. But... sometimes I can do just that."

He reaches then for the paper. He turns it over and I see, written there, the sum of money that I owe him. Then he speaks again, in a soft voice, "This is your debt. This is everything you have lost in my club. You cannot take my money and be clean. You cannot take it and preserve your *kibun*. But I can refuse to take yours."

With that, he lifts the paper and tears it in half.

I look at the torn paper. Then I look at the old man.

And then I bow my head in gratitude.

Calmly, and with a pride I have never felt before, I stand up and I walk out of the casino and onto the damp streets of Busan.

I am ready for the sweetness of freedom.

When the people emerge from Egypt, they are described as *Chamushim*. The word literally means 'fivers.' When we look at things related to the number five, there are few references. But one thing pops out: birds and insects and fish are created on the fifth day. Animals, and people, come on the sixth. In this context, a fiver is less developed than an animal. In this context, the people lack the responsibility and initiative of those who are free. The people have been broken by their oppressors.

When they emerge from the sea, they sing a song. The entire song is summarized by Miriam the prophetess in only one verse: "Sing to G-d because he is pride of prides. The horse and rider he throws into the sea."

Speaking of the French-Algerian conflict, Sartre once wrote: "To shoot down a European is to kill two birds with one stone, to destroy an oppressor and the man he oppresses at the same time: there remains a dead man and a free man."

The Jewish people suffered tremendously at the hands of the Egyptians. They became *chamushim* instead of normal people. Even in the face of the tremendous numerical superiority they had before entering the sea, they were unable to defend themselves. Moshe himself could not conceive of such a defense. Like the victim of rape, they were immobilized by the simple existence of their attacker. They could not sing. But when Hashem cast the horse and rider into the sea, He destroyed two people: he destroyed the domesticated horse the Jewish people had become and he destroyed the rider who had controlled them.

What emerged was a part way to a free people.

But only part way.

When the people come to Marah, the waters are bitter and undrinkable. When they are nearly overcome by their thirst, G-d commands Moshe to toss a tree into the waters. Then, the waters become sweet.

If we look at the symbolism of this story, a clear meaning arises. Waters in Torah symbolize spirituality and spiritual rejuvenation. On the other hand, trees are consistently identified as gifts of G-d – think of the Garden of Eden. By acting as commanded and putting one of G-d's gifts to us into the water, we make His spiritual waters sweet. To me, the symbolism is clear: by using G-d's gifts (the commandments), we can appreciate the sweetness of G-d's spirituality.

Like the mathematician in the casino, the people had never had freedom before. They had never had room for spirituality. Like those freed in Egypt or Romania or Haiti, they were not ready to receive it. They were frightened of it. They want to flee back to their oppression. They want to flee the power of decision.

But this is not Hashem's plan. Instead, like the old man in the casino, Hashem teaches them the first lesson of freedom: with righteous action, the taste of freedom can be sweet indeed.

From this baseline, the people are made ready to receive the Manna — the physical gifts of the Divine relationship. And from there they can become a source of spirituality themselves — like the rock that gives waters.

History has shown us that more often than not, freedom leads to horror. The Arab Spring has reminded us of this bitter reality. But it need not be so. By remembering the gift of Hashem's commandments, we can sweeten our spiritual waters.

And by remembering the gifts of Hashem's commandments, we can be blessed in all we do, and we can be a source of blessing unto the world.

Note, a graduate from a prominent North Korean university would be treated with great respect in the south. I took some liberties with this reality.

Yitro: Companions

I was eleven years old when I found the body. My parents insisted that us kids get involved in talking to strangers. They'd sign us up to raise money or sell cookies or even ask poll questions, door-to-door. At first, we were scared silly of the idea. I guess that was why they signed us up. But by the time we reached eleven, we were pretty confident and outgoing kids. We no longer shook in fear when we knocked on a new door. Instead, we realized what each door represented: a chance to meet somebody new.

I came to John Teller's door just like I would come to any other. I walked up the front path, got up on the deck and reached for the doorbell. It was a sunny day; I remember that well. But the deck wasn't sunny. It was covered in shade from the house itself. Oddly, the deck was shaded but the interior of the house was filled with sunlight. That's why, even though the glass was frosted, I could see a man laying on the floor inside.

My parents had also signed us up for the Boy Scouts (well, my sisters were Girl Scouts). I wasn't a very good Boy Scout so I kind of made up what I did next. I called 911 on my phone and then I broke the glass, reached in and opened the door. I ran to the man, ready to help. But he had passed long before I came up his front walk. As I waited for the emergency responders, I just sat there. And I saw the man had equipment – electronic equipment – stacked all over his house. It looked pretty cool. I remember looking at him then, and regretting I hadn't knocked on *this* door earlier.

An ambulance came, and then the coroner and then the police. They all asked me questions. And I told them what I knew. And then they took the man away. I asked when and where he'd be buried, and they gave me a number to call. Next of kin would be notified first, they would decide what would happen.

I called that day and then the next. And then the one after that. But it wasn't long before it was obvious that John Teller had no next of kin. He had no children, no siblings, no wife (ex or otherwise). John Teller had had no living parents. And he had no friends. Nobody came forward to claim him.

A Detective came by his house, and they found instructions. John Teller had paid for a burial plot and a funeral. He wasn't a young man, and he hadn't expected to live forever. Three days after he died, his body was released to a funeral home. I went to his burial. There was no minister, there were no mourners. There was only me and a couple of guys from the funeral service itself.

The man had had a will. The instructions he left asked that it be read aloud over his grave. And so it was: in one month, everything the man owned would be sent to the city dump. The house itself was a rental. As I listened, a sadness overcame me. In less than a month, nothing would remain of John Teller.

It was as if nobody had ever knocked on his door.

By the time I got home, I'd decided I wasn't going to let him simply disappear.

I started researching Mr. Teller. He'd been in the army, in Korea. He'd had jobs as a lowly technician at electronics companies. And he'd worked hard, very hard. But he kept his head down. I managed to track down some old colleagues. The few who remembered him said he didn't like to distract himself with useless conversation. He was, in fact, totally alone.

And then, fifteen years before I'd found him, he'd retired. I wondered what a man who lives for work does for retirement. I thought I knew the answer: he did something with electronics. I wondered what. Eventually, my curiosity overcame me. I needed to know what all the electronics were about. So, I snuck into his house and began to look around. I found piles and piles of circuit boards and wiring. Then, in his basement, I found a bookcase full of notebooks. Every book was in date order. Every book was labeled. Every book was filled with precise notes. I began to read. And before long I realized John Teller had been working on one thing his entire life: he had been working on building an interstellar communications device.

Amazingly, according to his notes, he'd succeeded. According to his notes, the black box sitting on his basement workbench was a functioning Neutrino Wave Propagation Device, or NWPD. It was no bigger than a desktop computer. He claimed it worked. He claimed it sent messages faster than the speed of light. He also acknowledged that he would never really know. It is almost impossible for us to detect, much less knowingly direct, the movement of neutrinos.

The device wasn't simply a black box that just sat there. It was connected to a laptop which controlled it using a simple application. You'd type in what you wanted to share and then enter the star coordinates. Then, borrowing from an add for a popular messaging service at the time, you'd 'close your eyes and think hopeful thoughts'. John Teller had added the last bit as a touch of humor.

With that, your message would *probably* be sent, undisturbed by anything along the way.

All that was needed on the other end was a civilization capable of hearing what was being said.

The notebooks claimed the device could receive messages as well. But John Teller had never received a message through it. Perhaps that's why, in recent years, his work had become bitter. All of his work, all of his singular dedication, had come to nothing.

In his eagerness to communicate with the stars, he had given up on reaching out to his fellow man.

In the process, he had been left with nothing at all.

I wanted to write a story about the man. So that is what I did. I wrote it and pitched it to everybody I could think of. But nobody was interested. When I got real explanations (which were rare), the reviewers said it was too fanciful or that I needed to work on my writing (I was only eleven). I recast it as an obituary for the local paper, but even they weren't interested. The man hadn't been important enough.

When the month had almost passed, I realized that everything was going to disappear. I realized there was only one thing I could still do.

In the middle of the night – before the movers came – I went to John Teller's house, broke in, and stole the NWPD.

When I got home, I booted up the laptop, copied the story onto it and then sent it, with a hopeful thought, to Proxima Alpha Centari.

If the Earth wouldn't remember him, maybe the stars would.

Then, I went to sleep.

Three hours later, I was woken up by the laptop. It had started playing a song: "Hello darkness my old friend" by Simon and Garfunkel. I shot up, looked at the screen and saw a message.

"We loved the story," the message said, "Do you have some more?"

At first, I was just confused. Was somebody pranking me? Was this a final joke? But nothing in John's notebooks suggested this much of a sense of humor. He had been deadly serious about this machine. And as far as I knew, no other humans could even sense neutrino wave-based messages.

I skipped school the next day, determined to get something more. It was a good time to knock on doors. You're more likely to meet retirees with time on their hands if you show up in the middle of the day. And then, for the hundredth time, I went out to knock on doors. This time, it was *just* to get to know somebody new. A few people thought I was trying to case their houses, but one let me in. She'd been a mathematician in college and then a waitress for the rest of her life. One of her children supported her in her old age.

I wrote up her story. I shared it with her. And then I sent it on the NWPD.

And three hours later, I got another reply. Another positive review. This one was signed "The Companions."

I kept going. I played hooky from school to get interviews. And then to do research. My parents had never suspected I wouldn't show up at school. When they caught on (the principal called them) they were shocked. They put it down to adolescence. But I told them the whole story; I even showed them the device. They were not supportive. That only changed when I finally convinced them to read some of the stories. The stories had literature and history and science and math and engineering. And they had humanity.

My parents loved them. They even pulled me from school so I could focus on my writing.

And that's what I did. For years to follow, I wrote stories. I never did find a publisher. Instead, I self-published collections of ordinary people living ordinary lives. I hoped they could catch on, but nobody bought them. Often times, even the people whose stories I wrote weren't interested. In the books, I wasn't private about the existence of the Companions. But nobody believed me. Nobody even cared enough to notice.

I didn't have any way to change that.

Fourteen years later, the world exploded.

Astronomers had noticed *something* shooting through our solar system. It wasn't detectable in the visible light spectrum, but all sorts of other detectors picked it up. Then the astronomers noticed something far more dangerous. The sun had released a massive solar flare. When the electro-magnetic radiation hit a few minutes later, satellite communications were knocked out, computers were fried and – on the dayside of the earth – a huge part of the atmosphere was simply burned away. We didn't know it until later, but over a billion people had been killed. We had been attacked. We had no idea *who* had attacked us, but I had an idea *why*. Somebody other than the Companions had heard my messages. The very idea of it was like a punch to my gut.

We were warned then, using shielded emergency communications systems (and old-fashioned word of mouth), that should another flare hit we were to hide in basements or old municipal shelters. If we had oxygen, we were to bring it with us. We would have only seconds to react. Then, almost twelve hours later, the air raid sirens went off. I didn't know it then, but the same pattern had been observed. An unusual *something* was detected shooting towards the sun. Only this time, *my* side of the Earth was exposed. As everybody ran to whatever shelter they could find, I knew we couldn't survive another hit.

I ran to the NWPD, and I called for help.

The flare never came. Instead, within moments the sky darkened, the sun vanished, and the flare was replaced by some weird throbbing darkness. I guessed it was some kind of shield, rapidly constructed to protect us. It worked.

I was blown away by how quickly our situation had changed, by how quickly the Companions had come.

Billions were not killed on our side of the planet. But the atmosphere, globally, had thinned. Aircraft couldn't fly and neither could birds. The Far East had literally been burned. Aid convoys were sent out, but they would take months to reach the hardest hit areas.

Even where we were, lives were in shambles. The weak had died from the sudden change in oxygen levels. At our altitude (I lived in Colorado), it was even worse. Of course, the economy was badly damaged. The loss of so many communication devices had undermined trade and commerce. With all the social media it can be hard to remember that food is a part of commerce.

The world was in a state of shock. Nothing like this had ever occurred before. I was in a state of shock. My messages may have triggered the deaths of untold numbers of people.

But I kept writing stories. I couldn't think of anything else to do. As much destruction as I may have caused, I was also the only person who offered a path to redemption. I knew the Companions had saved us, and I knew I needed to give them what they wanted. And they wanted stories.

For three days, we were blind and increasingly desperate. But then our satellite systems suddenly started working again. And our TVs and phones and computers began to operate. Nobody understood why they suddenly worked. But just like that, we could see the devastation in Asia. As we watched, huge packages started falling from the sky. People in India, China and Afghanistan recovered them and found food and water inside. We watched it all, beamed live from our phones. We all knew *somebody* was helping us. *I* was the only one who knew who.

Then, we saw them. They were new points of light in the night sky. New stars that had never been there before. They formed a constellation – spaced evenly throughout our sky. The world exploded in conversation and analysis and conjecture. Had we been attacked? Had we been rescued?

As a planet, we watched and waited – wondering what would happen next. Then they came. Not a fleet of them, just one ship; one ship no larger than Volkswagen Bug. Despite its size, the astronomers and the military men saw it coming.

They debated attacking it. They debate greeting it with a parade. In the end, they just watched, almost immobilized by fear and uncertainty.

When it landed, it touched down at 454 Filbert Drive, Boulder, Colorado. It touched down in my front driveway. Social media connected the dots before the doors of the craft even opened. A few quick searches online and all my books were visible. Anybody could see the dedications to the space aliens I claimed to know. I must have made a billion dollars in those first few minutes. Everybody bought my books. I thought about people reading them. But I knew that when they did, they wouldn't learn about the Companions. Instead, they'd learn about each other.

As the earth watched, the little spacecraft just sat there. No creatures emerged from it. None came to speak to me. Then, after five minutes, it just shot back into the sky.

That was the last day I knocked on other people's doors. That was the first day people started knocking on mine.

People came to me, and I talked to them. With each interview a pattern grew stronger and stronger. They felt weak and exposed. They felt irrelevant. They felt tiny. And they wanted me to beam their stories to the sky. They wanted me to immortalize them just as I'd first done for John Teller.

I soon found myself spending every waking hour talking and writing. People wanted their stories told. I wanted, desperately, to tell them. TV crews hung out outside my house, constantly watching my upstairs bedroom. People commented on my health and my stamina. They read every word I wrote. While I was the greatest possible celebrity, I didn't write about celebrities.

I wrote about ordinary people.

Politicians came, of course. Some wanted their stories told. Others wanted their photos taken. All wanted to be close to me. They wanted some of my fame, some of my aura. But I didn't have time for them. I had more important things to do. I had stories to write. I had people's lives to share.

When Teri Vanderhouven showed up, I wanted her to go away, like all the rest. Everybody knew who she was. She too was 32. She (too) was a self-made billionaire. And she too traded in stories. But where I wrote them, she transmitted them. She had invented an instant messaging platform like no other. It was a little texting device with a highly sensitive remote EEG sensor. You'd type in your message and then, to send the message, you'd close your eyes and think a particular kind of thought. Happy, sad, hopeful – there were a few choices. The device would pick up your basic emotion and your message would go with some emotional baggage attached. Hers was the advertisement John Teller's manual had been referring to.

I didn't intend to let her in. I didn't care how rich she was. I didn't even care that John had referenced her work in his manual. The fact was, my parents let her in. Yes, I was still living with them. With all the stories I'd been writing, I'd never had a chance to move out.

I guess they thought she'd be good for me.

She came up to my room, pushed open my door, closed the curtains on my window, turned to me and said one thing: "6 billion."

"What?" I asked, already annoyed at her being there.

"There are over 6 billion people on this planet."

"So?" I said.

"If you write two stories a month, you'd be able to cover them all in about 250 million years."

I just looked at her. I had no idea what she was getting at.

"The Companions," she said, "Want stories. Stories of ordinary people. You can't possibly deliver them."

"So, what I am supposed to do?" I asked. I'd never really thought about the question.

Her answer was simple. Others would write as well. I would choose ten authors, people who weren't seeking their own fame but who truly wanted to tell the stories of others. I would write about them. Then they would choose ten others. Then those hundred would choose another thousand. Until more than 10% of humankind was writing and *everybody* was being written about. When big stories

71

were found, they would be sent up the pyramid until a writer felt capable of handling them. The biggest of all would flow all the way to me.

I took her idea. I changed it, but I took it. Instead of writing the biggest stories, I would write the *hardest* stories. A nobody, a 'small' person, could make for the greatest of tales.

From that day onwards, we began to work together. She copied the design of the NWPD and new systems were placed all over the world. Then we all started broadcasting, together, the stories of humankind.

200 stories a second were shot into the space around us.

In the process, a remarkable thing happened. As we wrote, we were knit together. We no longer felt so weak and alone. And we began to grasp for the stories of those around us. As we wrote, the Companions began to come in greater and greater numbers. Their few points of light in our sky began to spread. Thousands and thousands and thousands more arrived. Soon, the Earth was bathed in the glow of their illumination.

We knew, we could feel, that something great was coming.

Then the Companions spoke back. Through every NWPD on the planet, they told us to be ready for a great change. They told us the minute it would come. At dusk in my hometown in three days. You could touch the excitement. As the time drew near, the Earth seemed to come to a stop. People gathered together, holding hands, talking – appreciating the stories of others, even if they were not writing them down.

Millions of people came to *my* city. They seemed to fill every available space, and even poured up the slopes of the mountains on the western flank of Boulder. As the sun drew down, they were captured by the shade of the peaks. They were all waiting for the hour of change.

Then, right on schedule, it happened.

From the skies above, a billion billion billion voices began to share their stories. Not in a white noise, but individually. We heard them in our heads, all simultaneously, filling our minds with the vastness of the universe. I reveled in it, filled with the joy of lives lived.

But here, *I* was alone.

Outside my house, a great terror arose. All around the world, the people screamed and begged for the stories to stop. There were too many. It was too much. They could not survive the onslaught. They were overcome by terror.

And so, I typed into the NWPD, and I asked the stories to stop.

And, just like that, they did.

Then the crowds waited in anticipation. Nobody knew what would happen next. The minutes passed. And then I *felt* a story in my head. It was not in any language I could understand, but I understood it, nonetheless.

I began to write. This time, I was not writing the stories of humanity for the sake of the heavens above; I was writing the stories of heaven for the sake of mankind.

People went back to their lives. They went back to writing their stories. They read every word I shared.

And the glow of the skies remained, promising our transformation when we were finally strong enough to grasp it.

Until then, I've got a billion billion billion stories still to share.

Most see the delivery of the *Aseret Hadibrot* (Ten Commandments) as the highlight of our relationship with G-d. I see it a little differently. We were told to prepare for *Bimshoch HaYovel*. *Bimshoch* comes from *hemshech*. In modern Hebrew, the root means 'to continue.' But in Biblical Hebrew, that translation would be senseless. Aside from the naming of a descendent of Yapheth, the word only occurs twice. The first is before the bringing of the Pascal lamb. Just before they are to actually get the lambs, the people are told "*mashcho* and get lambs". The second is here. There are various possible translations of this word, but few can bridge both situations. I believe a good translation would be "transform."

With the taking of the Pascal lamb, the people transform into G-d's nation.

At Har Sinai, they have the opportunity to transform once again.

Where the people were made into G-d's people at the time of Exodus, here they are to step into the *Yovel*. The *Yovel* is the Jubilee. It is a time in which loss and risk are eliminated. It is a time, like in Eden, in which we do not need to build and invest to stop decay; but can build and invest purely to touch the timeless. We can create, not to hold back destruction, but for its own sake. Reaching the *Yovel* requires trust. After all, with the *Yovel*, the nation will have two years without crops. Nothing will be harvested or planted during the Yovel and so nothing will be harvested in the year that follows. If the nation has trust, then G-d promises that crops will increase in anticipation of the *Yovel*.

If they don't, then the *Yovel* will be beyond them.

With *Bimshoch HaYovel*, the people are to step into this timeless reality. They were meant to be able to ascend the mountain and approach G-d. But to do it, they needed trust. When the time came, the people did not have trust. They shook in terror. Theirs was not the fear of G-d, but a lack of trust in Hashem.

Instead of ascending the mountain, we receive commandments, commandments that set the baseline of our relationship with G-d and with each other.

I borrowed these ideas for this story. Like G-d, the Companions want to relate to us. Like G-d, they are too vast for us to integrate with. Moshe's first recorded actions were as a judge. He may or may not have been the best of judges, but at least he tried. He took responsibility. The storywriter is the same. He may not be the best writer, but at least he tried to record the story of a forgotten man.

In the end, both take on responsibility for vast numbers of people. And both are near being overcome by their obligations.

In Moshe's story, Yitro appears. His credentials get him an audience with a very busy man. He suggests a system of judgment. It not only helps Moshe and enables justice; it also fills the people with *responsibility*. Likewise, Teri's advice not only helps the storywriter; it also fills the world with *appreciation*. In both cases, the *possibility* of transformation is created by the change in the people.

Of course, in the end, there is no fundamental change.

We are not drawn into the *Yovel* or made into Companions. We are not ready for that sort of change. In the Torah's story, we receive law from above to complement the growth of justice from below. Amazingly, the system of judges is the only mitzvah to come purely from mankind. In the case of the Companions, we receive stories from above to complement those that come from below.

In both cases, the possibility of transformation remains. It hovers in the heavens above, ready to welcome us when we are ready. Even today, a transformation of our reality remains within reach.

A whole new world awaits our responsibility, our mutual appreciation, and our trust.

Mishpatim: Boulevard

A light rain has lifted the oily discharge of 10,000 motors off the surface of the Boulevard. The oils shine in the streetlights and flash with the lights of the passing cars. They grant the asphalt a constantly shifting rainbow hue. Their smell rises up from the road and mixes with the exhaust of the cars, filling the air with a gritty scent.

As the cars pass by, *all* their drivers seem to notice me. I can't blame them. I'm standing under a streetlamp in cheap high heels and a cheaper mini-skirt. I am meant to be noticed.

Many who pass stare at me with open contempt. I stare back at them, defiant. Others, men and even a few women, glance guiltily in my direction as they speed by. Still others have eyes that seem to consume me. But I don't need eyes. I need money. $50 ought to do it.

I watch everyone's faces as they pass, feeling strangely at home as they look at me. This is my first night on the street and yet it seems like my whole life has led me here.

I see a pasty-white woman zoom by in a late-model minivan. She's probably running home from some late-night soccer game. She glances at me and in that instant, I see a look I know too well. My first memory is of that look. It is my mother's look: supportive, caring and hopeful. But underneath it is something else.

More cars zoom by.

I'm a thin woman, eaten away by drugs. I know I don't look good, but I try to keep my hopes up. I know there is risk to what I'm doing. I know junkies must attract the worse kind of clientele.

But I don't show my fear and I've long since lost my shame.

Instead, my face stretched thin by malnourishment, I try my best to give the Boulevard what it wants.

My parents were pasty white people. They lived the middle-class dream. They had a home, a yard, everything. But everything was surrounded by middle-class responsibilities, and middle-class fears. They may not have said it, but all anybody cared about was what other people thought. They were prisoners in a carpeted cage.

I wasn't like them, and I'd always known it. My earliest memory was of trying on my mom's makeup in front of her mirror. I put it on the way *I* liked it – thick and loud. My mother caught me, of course. I saw her looking at me through the mirror. That was when I saw that look in her eyes. It was supportive, caring and hopeful. But there was something else. It might have been disappointment. It might have been fear.

I was already a wild child.

My parents wanted to limit my worst impulses, but they didn't exactly hold the line. It wasn't that they were weak (or that I was stubborn). Instead, they had a philosophical objection to constraining me. I was raised in a house with no 'negative' energy. They believed, deeply, that I needed to express my true self. They believed that, given enough love, everything would turn out well. That belief was shallower than they would ever have admitted, *especially* to themselves. I could see it in their eyes.

They wanted me to be a free spirit, but they didn't like what they saw when I was.

As soon as I could put form to the fear, I realized they were afraid I'd be a street kid. They were afraid I'd do drugs. They were afraid I'd sell my body.

All that expectation was waiting for me.

As I grew older, the expectation spread. Childhood friends acquired it. They drifted away. Elementary school teachers acquired it. They focused on other children. By the time I was thirteen, I was hanging out with a rough crowd, and I was the roughest of them all.

My parents, my teachers, my oldest friends? They saw nothing in me and all I wanted to do was get away from them. I hated my world, and I hated my life. My parents would ask where I'd been and what I'd done, and I'd lie. They put trackers on my phone, and I uninstalled them. They didn't let me have cash, so I stole it from them. They even locked their medicine cabinet, which is when I figured out that *that* was where I wanted to be. They wanted me to join them in their carpeted cage, but I wasn't going to allow it.

I wanted to be free. And my friends, my real friends, made me feel that way. We'd get together and we'd do *whatever* we wanted. I'd get home at 3 or 4 in the morning. I'd be drunk or high. And while my parents and my teachers knew what I was doing, they never said anything about it. Nothing real, anyway. They all *said* they expected more from me. I knew they really didn't.

I was no longer a disappointment. I was an accepted reality.

They wanted a free spirit, and that's what they had.

I left home when I was sixteen. My parents made all the right, pro-forma, objections. Secretly, though? They were delighted. They could just say I had just gone off to discover myself. They could tell everybody about their free-spirited daughter's return in a few years, with a few grand adventures under her belt. They were sure I would grow up. In the meantime, they didn't have to deal with me. Best of all, nobody in the community would be talking about their daughter.

When I moved out, I didn't exactly travel the world. Instead, I carried a single bag to a massive and growing homeless camp on the east side of town. Some of my friends were already there.

Some tent cities had rules and a curfew. Those places were for people who couldn't afford rent. They were for people who wanted to be a part of the world. They were for people who dreamed of a carpeted cage.

We also couldn't afford rent, but that wasn't *why* we were there. We were there because *we were free*. The rest of humanity was a bunch of mindless robots, *programmed* by the world around them. Society made them dance like little puppets. But *we were free*. We alone made our own choices. We alone were *real*. Unlike all the simulations of humanity we'd abandoned, we felt *real* joy and *real* pain – not some carpeted version of true emotions.

We had the guts to truly live life.

It wasn't easy though. Society is all about protecting society. It can't let people like us really be free, or others might escape, and everything would break down. So, the police would hassle us. They'd arrest loiterers, or rampage through our homes or roust those sleeping on benches. Maybe some of them thought they were helping us. But we knew better. They were just doing what society wanted. They were trying to make us conform.

They were attacking us because our way of life *upsets* theirs. Our choices forced them to confront the hollowness of their own lives.

I guess that's where I got the attitude from. Whenever some buttoned-up stick of person looked down on me, I looked right back at them. Society was trying to judge us, but society was nothing.

We dealt in reality. We lived in reality.

They were the ones trying to hold reality at bay.

Of course, repression didn't stop with the cops. When it came time for the distribution of wealth, society tried to cut us out. They wouldn't let us have our fair share. We protested. We stole. We sold drugs to the proper people's children. But even so, things were tight.

There were limits to what we could get our hands on.

And I was beginning to need more than I ever had before. I used to just enjoy the painkillers, but now I *needed* pills to feel anything but pain. I started skipping meals, so I'd have enough money to buy them. It wasn't enough; drugs were more expensive than food.

I started spending time with men I barely knew. I started partying with them and taking advantage of the drugs and alcohol they all seemed to have for me. I tried to tell myself I liked the attention. I thought maybe I could lie a smile back into my heart. But they knew and I knew that we were engaged in a far simpler transaction.

It worked for a while though. I got what I needed. But then they started to turn me away; I was too well-known a commodity. Too well used.

Soon, I was hanging out on the fringes of the tent city. I was on the edge of even my civilization. I tried to convince myself that I was just free of another society; I was just free of another kind of repression. But I knew it wasn't so. I was trapped within myself; buried by my own freedoms.

I was done.

It was there, hanging out on the edge of that camp, that I decided my end had come. I would spend everything I had on one final dose. An overdose. I'd buy 5 Fentanyl patches. It would cost me $50. I'd use them all at once. And I'd leave this world feeling good.

All I needed was the $50.

I knew I could get it on the Boulevard. I thought I knew it. It seems like, even here, I can't seem to catch a break.

And then I see it. A beautiful car cruising down the street. Is it a Bentley? I watch in shock as it pulls up next to me. A window rolls down and I walk up to it, flaunting what little I have. Then I look inside and see the face of a woman.

Her eyes lock with mine in an expression I've never seen before.

"How much?" the woman asks. She's wearing incongruous clothes; a tee-shirt and a hoodie.

"$50," I say. I don't want to ask for more than I need. I don't want to risk not getting it.

"Get in," says the woman. She snaps her finger and the driver's side door opens. A huge man emerges. He is hulking and frightening, and I look at him in absolute terror. I suddenly don't want to get into *that* car. I don't understand what the woman wants.

I shudder. The man stops.

I look back at the woman. I can't read her expression. I can't place it. She *is* in a Bentley though. She must have money. And I need money.

Steeling myself, I lean towards the window, letting the woman see as much as she'd like. But she only looks at my eyes. And then, she looks away. In a loud voice, she pronounces three words: "Mark, let's go."

My hands are still on the window as the car begins to pull away. As desperate as I am, I can't hold on for long, though. I let go. I watch the car roll away and it seems like I've got nothing left.

A minute later, Mark, the woman and the Bentley are gone.

I stumble back from the street and towards the façade of a building. There, I just collapse. I fall to the ground hungry and tired and fundamentally exhausted.

I wake up the following morning. I do wake up. And when I do, there's an large, padded envelope in my hand.

I look at it through bleary eyes. I don't understand what it is, not at first. An envelope is so incongruous I can hardly imagine it being there. Eventually, I pull it open.

There are only two things inside. a credit card and a note. I pull the note out and read it:

The credit card has $100 on it. Buy breakfast and then a bus ticket. Go anywhere small. Once there, go online (I suggest the library). If you visit the following address, I'll add another $100 to the credit card.

– the woman in the car

A URL follows the note. I just stare at it, trying to work out what this crazy woman wants to do to me. I'm trying to work out how she is going to torture me. But I can't figure it out.

I get up from my stoop and then I head to an ATM. I'll get the cash and then I'll disappear.

I consider buying the drugs I wanted just a few hours before. I still want them. My body is wracked with pain. But I don't want to die, not yet. I spend $20 on a patch – a real rip-off. I stick it on, the feeling of relief is immediate. Then I spend $10 on cheap snacks at a convenience store. And then I find myself heading to one of those on-the-street intercity bus stops. Maybe I'll see where this road goes? Or maybe I'll go back to the dealer and finish myself off.

I'm curious, though. And so, as each bus stops, I ask the drivers what small towns they might stop at. They tell me. And I listen. And I realize that I can choose where I'm going to go.

I have just a little bit of freedom. Perhaps my life is not yet over.

I finally pick a place and buy a ticket. I spend $65. I've got almost nothing left.

As the bus pulls away, I drift off in a stupor. Eight hours later, the driver drops me off in what seems like the middle of nowhere. The place is a small town, the kind of place I'd only ever driven through during insufferable family vacations designed to gather photos for my parents' friends.

The town has a main drag with low-slung buildings running down either side of it. There are a few traffic lights and angled parking on either side of the street. Half the shops seem boarded up. The other half have "Help Wanted" signs plastered on them. The place seems dead.

I look around until I figure out where the library is. Then, I head there.

It is time to collect my next $100.

There's no wait for a computer, not like in the city. There's just a woman who looks at me with baleful eyes. Just like everybody else does. But she lets me use the computer. I go to the address from the note and there's another message waiting for me.

The card now has another $100. If you want more, you must do the following. First, you have to pull a fingernail out each and every time you use. Second, in two days you have to visit this address again, from your current location. Do those two things, and another payment awaits you.

-- The woman in the car

I stare at the screen. My first thought is anger. Who is this woman to tell me what to do? And how could she possibly enforce what she's asking for? I could spend all the money on drugs and then come back here and she'd never know. That's actually what I plan on doing. I log out, stand up from the desk and storm out of the library. The librarian seems relieved to see me go.

But once I'm outside, a thought occurs to me. The woman *can't enforce what she's asking for*.

Instead, she's *trusting* me to do it myself. Her calculus seems pretty brutal. If I harm myself, I have to harm myself. But I know it can work. The thought of pulling a nail out reviles me even more than the thought of needles once did.

I commit, then and there, to her demands.

I don't bother converting the card to cash. I'll let her watch what I do. I'll let her confirm I can be trusted. I find a diner; I buy myself dinner. It is the best I've eaten in months. I rent a room at a cheap motel. It is the nicest place I've stayed at in over a year. My whole body hurts, I miss the patches, but I make it through the next two days, somehow.

I do make it, barely. Shaking with the pain of withdrawal, I come back to the library. There is another $100 waiting for me. And another note.

The fingernail rule still applies, but this time the woman insists that I walk. I have to walk five miles each day. It isn't easy. My body had been thrashed by my lifestyle. But I make it. Five miles each day. And I feel better for it.

There is $200 and another note. The rules are layered on. This time I have to "buy new clothes and keep them clean."

I visit the general story and I do what she asks. My clothes haven't been laundered in forever and so whatever cheap crap the store has is a big step up. I find myself dressing in tracksuit pants, a tee-shirt and a hoodie. They smell clean. I look a little less like a junkie.

Another $100. "Open a bank account."

Another $100. "Stay away from men. I can give you what you need."

I'm falling into a rhythm. I'm standing alone.

Another $200. "Give the waitress a huge tip."

She smiles, delighted with the $100 I leave her. I feel even better than she does.

Another $100. "Respect yourself."

I don't know what that means, but I realize it might actually be happening for the first time in my life.

Another $100. "Get a job." I apply at the diner. They accept me. They accept me!

Another $100. "Keep that job." I make sure to show up on time. And I do.

Another $100. "Trust your head, your heart wavers." I don't understand what she wants. But for the first time in my life, I begin to save my money.

I keep going every other day. As I do, the amount the woman gives me slowly falls away. $80, then $60, then $40, then $20 and then... nothing but a note.

A note without money. It has only one line:

Do something worthwhile with your life.

   – the women in the car.

I get up then and walk the streets of that small town. This is the biggest challenge of all. I have no idea what I should do. I keep working. I keep saving. In a few months, I have over $2000 in cash.

I look at the money one night. I just stare at it. It doesn't feel like a carpeted cage. The number rolls through my head. Then, with a jolt I realize something that shocks me. The woman had paid me to save myself. But all she gave me was $1400.

With $1400, she saved my life.

I head to the diner, and I ask the cook if he can do help me out. He's a brute of a man. Together we take a bus to the nearest city. We rent a luxury car. He drives.

And then we head for the nearest Boulevard.

I cruise the street, looking at the women selling themselves. And then I see her. She's standing there, looking like I must have. But when I look at her, I don't see what my mother saw, or what my teachers saw, or what my friends saw. I don't see the expectation of a short life ended by an overdose.

Instead, I see myself. I see a free woman. A strong woman.

A woman able to help another.

I roll down the window. The grit of the city seeps into the car.

The woman looks at me. She's confused. She's scared. She's never seen eyes like mine. She's never seen eyes that saw her potential instead of expecting her failure. She can get into the car. She can ride away with me. But she trembles and I know it is not meant to be.

As I pull away, I see her slump onto the sidewalk, just as I had done. We return the car. And in the middle of the night, the cook goes back.

He finds the woman sleeping. He slips an envelope under her hand.

In it is a credit card, a note, and the possibility of a new reality.

At the end of last week's Torah reading, the Jewish people are given the Ten Commandments. But there is a hint of something more being available. We are meant to come up the mountain. We are meant to experience *Bimshoch HaYovel*, which I translate as a fundamental transformation to the *yovel* – a reality in which, perhaps – we are no longer constrained from reality. But then, so afterwards, we are forbidden from ascending the mountain. We miss out on the *yovel*.

The question is, why? Reading the text, we see that *we* do only one thing between when we are supposed to ascend and when we are forbidden from doing so: we tremble in fear.

We have a chance for a fundamental change, but we are too frightened to accept it.

We do not *trust* Hashem.

As I understand it, that is the context of the laws in this reading. These laws are meant to teach us what Hashem seeks from us. They are meant to teach us *not* to be terrified of him. They are meant to build us up.

The process of being able to face Hashem – in fear but not terror – starts with understanding that He wants our potential to be maximized. Without will, we have no potential. This is why Hashem establishes laws that limit our slavery. They guarantee that society is never without its limits. And they show us that such limits come from G-d.

We can choose to reject our freedom, but when we do so we drive an awl through our ears and symbolically sever our connection to Hashem; our ability to hear Him. And, even when we do this, we are making a choice to do so.

In the story, the young woman decides where she wants to go. It is her first step towards freedom. It is the first step of her understanding that the woman in the car means to lift her up, not tear her down.

The laws continue. Threats to life are next. The loss of a life in a society damages it, just as the use of drugs damages a body. It is resisted through punishment, just as in the story. The laws continue, protecting our bodies (exercise) and then property (clothes) and then our future (the bank account). They then forbid us from worshiping other values (men). They insist we treat the weak well (waitress tip), respect judges (listen to our heads, not hearts), and build a relationship with Hashem through investment in Him (do something worthwhile with your life).

Step by step, the laws build us up. At the end of the Torah reading, we make a national offering – our first national offering – to Hashem. We ask to come close to Him, repeating that we will do, and we will listen. And He welcomes us. We sit before Him. We eat. We no longer tremble in terror. We have grown, and we have grown to understand.

And we are ready to build the house of G-d.

Terumah: Numbers

I open the door to my new office and step in. A cardboard box is in my hand. It has everything I need. I look at the room, with its two walls of tinted glass, its clean carpet and its massive desk. It smells of industrial carpet cleaner, generously applied. It seems to perfectly match the scent of my dry-cleaned suit.

I close the door behind me, so nobody can see me. Then I smile the broadest smile of my life.

I am finally where I belong.

I step forward and gingerly place the cardboard box on the clear table. I remove the lid and stare down at the contents. Leaning against one side is my laptop and power cord. I remove it and place it on the desk in front of my office chair. I line it up perfectly with the desk and run the wire through to the power port. I take a moment to examine my handiwork and then I return to the box.

I pull out a single sheet of laminated paper. I place it, face up, exactly two inches from the corner of the desk. It will be on the near right corner for those who enter my office. It too is lined up with the desk. On the paper, I place an empty pill bottle, a candy bar with a sale sticker on it and a napkin with a diagram jotted down. All are lined up with one another, perpendicular to my laptop so that I can see them easily when I work.

Finally, at the bottom of the box is a collection of over 1000 letters. They come in all shapes and sizes and colors. I pick them out, one by one, and slowly and methodically tape them to my new office walls. I line them up in a pattern I laid out on my computer before coming here.

It has taken me all day, but I am finally done. I lift the box from the table and place it near the door. Then I turn around and look again at the space.

My laptop is in position, but more importantly so are the other objects: the paper, candy car, pill bottle, napkin and letters.

I smile again. This *is* where I belong.

When I was in grade school, I wanted to fit in. I never managed to do so. When troupes of girls would start obsessing over fashion or a band or even one another, I would *try* to get involved. I would read up on the subject and maybe watch a video or two. I would prepare a few comments so I could seem to be interested. Then, when I got a chance, I'd join in a conversation. I'd say my piece. But moments later, invariably, everybody would either laugh at me or drift away.

I'd go home and cry. And then I'd try again. I'd adjust my approach, of course. I'd analyze the probabilities of different elements combining to realize the desired outcome: popularity, or at least acceptability.

Time after time, I'd keep trying. Time after time, I'd keep failing.

It seemed I didn't know how to communicate with my peers.

It took me a while to realize that the real problem was that *they* didn't know how to communicate with *me*. I didn't realize that they were *really* interested in the band or the fashion or how they did their hair. I thought they were just pretending. I thought it was all some sort of social dance necessary to achieve popularity. I thought it was a means to an end. I didn't realize the dance itself was the point.

I thought, I truly believed, that they were like me. I thought they saw the world as numbers and patterns and geometric relationships. I thought they watched others walk and pulled out patterns in their

91

movements. I thought they also saw equations in their movements through the playground; in the ways they clumped and shifted. I thought they thought like I did.

But they didn't.

It turned out I even dreamed differently than they did. Where they dreamed in images, I dreamed in formulas and integers and geometric relationships.

I had nothing in common with them. I was *different* from them. Over time, I pulled away from them. What I was interested in, they could not understand. It seemed like the inverse was also true.

As I grew older, the differences only grew starker. As a child I *consumed* numbers. I read mathematics textbooks. I saw patterns around me. Bit by bit, though, I began to *create* in numbers. Just as an artist would bring an image to life on a canvas, or a writer in words, I began to create in numbers. Patterns would speak to me, telling stories – capturing beauty only I seemed able to see and revealing truths others wanted to hide. I went through college this way. I got a degree in mathematics, of course. The coursework wasn't what kept me busy, though. It was simple. Far more of my time was spent conjuring numerical realities that nobody but I seemed capable of appreciating.

I loved what I was doing. I loved the beauty of it. I loved the complexity. I loved the honesty. I didn't need to go to college for any of it, though. I knew the math and I loved the numbers. I didn't belong there, and I knew it. I wasn't doing what I was meant for, and I knew it.

The one thing college gave me, that my art could not, was a job. My senior year, a professor of mine found me a position. I was to be an analyst at the state government employee pension fund.

I expected I'd find my tribe there among other analysts. I hoped to find my purpose and my home.

But I didn't. I didn't know it at the time, but when I was hired, I was hired as a 'diversity' employee. I was considered disabled; autistic to be precise. I didn't think I was disabled, but I did end up filling some sort of state quota. It was why I got the job. The fund was happy to hire me. People felt good having me around. But nobody *really* expected me to contribute much of anything. I was supposed to run routine reports and present them to management. I wasn't meant to be tasked with anything too difficult. Of course, the jobs of my coworkers weren't that much more advanced – although they may have disagreed.

It was *all* basic stuff done by basic people. Sure, the people were geekier than the average, but even they didn't see the world the way I did. I was far from fulfilled.

The job turned from okay to worse when my managers started explaining pension accounting to me. It didn't take me long to 'get' what they were explaining. But I could not accept it. It seemed like the accounting was just 'corrections' piled on top of corrections. Excessively optimistic projections were combined with theoretical future makeup of shortfalls which were themselves additionally enhanced. The rise in healthcare costs was forecasted to become something magically brought under control. And all of it was combined to make a system that was terribly broken seem less so. Even with all the lies, it didn't work. What we published were projections of shortfalls that were themselves incredibly optimistic. I was hired to help them lie.

I couldn't accept making the numbers lie. To me numbers were beauty, and their beauty was being rotted away. I tried to bury my head. I tried to pretend it wasn't happening. But I couldn't. I could see the lies, the corruption of the truth of numbers, spreading. I could see pensioners and then society being slowly overwhelmed by the truth the numbers told. I could see everything falling apart.

Hunger in the streets. Elderly homelessness. Lack of medicines. All numbers as promises that turned out to be lies.

And there was nothing I could do.

After I understood the problem, I spent every waking hour thinking about it. I wanted to *solve* it. But I kept coming back to two realities. Either the truth of the numbers was accepted (in which case people's lives unraveled now as the promises made to them shrank massively under their very eyes). Or the lies were continued, promises were paid out and those paid last were left with nothing at all.

There seemed to be no other options.

Even the greatest mathematician couldn't stop it. All they could hope to do was slow it down.

It all seemed so hopeless. I gave up.

Then, I was diagnosed with cancer.

When I took a leave of absence, my co-workers pitied me; like I had suffered so much, only to suffer this as well. I can't say, at that point, that I disagreed with them. But what bothered me most of all wasn't my own suffering or death; it was the gaping lie I was threatening to leave behind. It was the great unsolved equation that I could not understand or conquer.

The doctors tried chemotherapy and radiation and surgery. I watched as my odds of survival shifted and wandered. They jerked and spasmed at first. But then slowly they settled down. As I got sicker and sicker, my diagnosis got clearer. The numbers were not good. I was hopeless and it seemed like the best it could do was slow things down, a bit.

As the cancer continued to rage through me, I began to see it like I saw the accounting. Chemotherapy might slow the cancer down – just like cutting benefits would – but the body would suffer terribly. The alternative would just encourage the runaway costs and when the end came it would be far more sudden.

Neither one was a winner.

Then I was entered into a trial for an immunotherapy treatment. The results were amazing. Within weeks, I was in complete remission. A few days after that, I was back at work. I was effectively cured. My own cells had been given the tools to rescue me.

I started to think of the fund's problems as a cancer. Perhaps, I imagined, some sort of immunotherapy would help. Instead of trying to force solutions from on high and trying to chase down individually replicating costs with roughly applied controls that damaged innovation and limited care, maybe something else could be done. Maybe individuals could somehow be used to drive down their own costs. Maybe, somehow, they could be empowered to create better outcomes; like white blood cells being trained to chase down a cancer.

But I didn't know how to do it. I threw myself into the problem, but I had no practical ideas.

It was while I was having coffee at a café – alone – that I got my answer. A mother came and sat down near me. She had her son with her.

The boy gestured towards the convenience store next door and asked, "Can I have a treat?"

The mother said, "Here are two dollars. Buy whatever you want. Oh, and keep the change."

The boy ran off like a shot. I was curious what would happen, so I stayed even after I finished my coffee. A few minutes later, the kid ran back – almost out of breath. In one hand, he held a candy car. It was marked with a prominent 'Half Price' sticker. In the other he held a receipt. He was proud, and he'd be taking home 75 cents in change.

The boy hadn't had to pay for his treat. But he'd been frugal, and he'd done his tiny part in driving down the cost of candy.

That was the cure I was looking for. Instead of bombarding our members with cost controls, we could empower them. If they were brought in with a suspected lump, we would figure out the median cost of getting to the next diagnosis. And then, just like the mother did, we'd pay them a bit more than that. They'd shop around for a diagnosis and keep the change. Then, they'd get to the next step. Perhaps it would be another diagnosis, with another traunch of money following to treat whatever they had. Advanced models and huge amounts of patient data would take the factors of their situation into account to determine what the mean was, and how much needed to be paid. Open, anonymous, records, would enable diagnosis to be checked by freelance auditors. Finally, we'd keep receipts of whatever they spent on their care – so we could update the median cost. But they, the patients, would keep the change.

The fund was so large, and had so many patients that each of them, with each choice, would drive down the cost of care. The median cost of treatments would drop year after year, as providers competed for business. Our patients would be frugal, and providers would cut costs in order to get their business.

Just as important, *we* would meet our promises to them. They'd get enough money to treat their diagnosis. We wouldn't leave them uncared for.

There would be no lies in our numbers.

I grabbed a napkin from the holder, and I began to chart the effects. I couldn't do it perfectly; you can't really predict innovation. But there are standard models. I could see costs plummeting while services improved – just like in high-tech or in laser eye surgery. New incentives would ripple through the system and rebuild it from the ground up. The fund might just survive.

I ran to the store and bought another of the candy bars. And then I ran back to work. I skipped my desk. I skipped my manager. I just burst into the office of the man who ran the entire thing. He looked up at me. And then I held up the candy bar and I explained my idea.

He was a numbers guy. *He* got it. *He* made it happen.

Signatures had to be gathered, a vote had to be held. People needed to be convinced. But *he* made it happen. And soon, it was the way the fund managed its healthcare expenses. It worked even better than I thought it would.

Indian providers – Indian! – got into the market for our patients. They offered high quality surgeries at low prices and our patients responded. Local providers got more competitive. Clinics opened in the Bahamas. High tech got into the act. New therapies were designed – therapies designed to save money. Innovation, in delivery, in administration, in technology – exploded.

Costs, suddenly under pressure from a sort of social immunotherapy, plummeted. In the end, the fund was rescued. The lies were unwound.

Truth came back to the numbers.

A newspaper interviewed me about what I'd done. I told them the story. Then, the letters started coming in. They were letters of gratitude and of thanks. They were letters about worries lifted and fears erased. I read each of them. I didn't stop there, though. I calculated their count and colors and content, and I put them up in ordered rows; bringing some bit of organization to their beautiful variety. I covered my cubicle in neatly arranged layers of letters.

Finally, I was promoted.

I was made a fund manager.

I wasn't the top dog; I would never be a politician. But I was something close.

I was being recognized. I was being appreciated.

I was finally being welcomed.

As I walked into my new office, my little cardboard box was with me. I unpacked it carefully, treating each item reverentially.

The pill box used to contain a part of *my* immunotherapy. It told me the concept I must aspire to.

The candy bar was the one I bought on sale from the store. It told me *how* I could make the concept real.

The napkin was the one I wrote on in the café, it was the revelation of what I was possible.

Together, they are the reasons I am where I am.

I had placed all the items on the laminated paper. The paper is a print-out of rule changes the fund members voted for. They are what made the revelation a reality.

And the letters, the letters taped to the walls are the thanks I have received. They reveal the beauty of what I have discovered.

I look it all over then and I smile yet again.

I have a new job. Here, sitting at this desk, I will take the ideas of others and I will figure out how to make them real. I will empower the members of our fund. I will be the beating heart of our organization.

I smile once more, truly happy.

My office is a tabernacle of financial immunotherapy.

Finally, I turn around and purposefully pull open the door. It is time to get to work.

I have a purpose, finally, to fulfill.

This week's Torah reading lays out the plan of the Mishkan (Tabernacle). G-d tells the people he wants to dwell within them. The Mishkan is a literal expression of this.

The three symbolic objects capture G-d's revelations to the people. The burning bush is represented by the Menorah – which burns and is never consumed. It gave Moshe the ideological target of creation without destruction. The Mahn (Manna) is represented by the table with its showbread, literally the 'bread of faces' through which G-d's presence is revealed. And the Ark represents the great revelation at Mount Sinai, where the presence of G-d was truly understood.

Together they represent the presence of Hashem.

Each is represented, in a way, by the little items on our heroine's desk. The pill box represents the ideological target (G-d's ideology, in the Menorah). The candy the basic concept (G-d's presence, in the show bread). And the napkin the great revelation (the way to make G-d's presence a part of our lives, the Ark).

The Mishkan doesn't stop there. G-d says he wants the people to be a *Mamlechet Kohanim* (Kingdom of Priests) and *Goy Kadosh* (Holy people).

A Kingdom has rules and laws, and priests draw close to G-d. This is why the Mishkan has pillars covered with curtains to form walls. There are 53 inner pillars and 56 external ones (excluding the separate gate). In the previous reading of Mishpatim, there are 53 socially enforced laws and 56 possible outcomes (three laws have two possible paths that can be chosen). The laws enable the people to drive out destruction – and thus draw close to G-d. The pillars represent the laws upheld by the people just as the rule changes on the laminated sheet do. They represent the *Mamlechet Kohanim*.

Finally, the inner pillars are covered by cloth with images of *Keruvim* – angels close to G-d – woven into them. The word *goy* is not like Mamlechet, it doesn't unite people through rules or a ruler. It is relatively formless, but still distinct. The soft curtains represent the *Goy Kadosh*; less structured but identifiable and close to G-d. The letters from fund members offer related symbolism, unstructured and yet Holy.

With this layout, G-d's revelations are held within the people's walls. G-d's literal representation dwells within the representation of the people as *Mamlechet Kohanim* and *Goy Kadosh*. G-d dwells within the people.

Of course, the Mishkan doesn't stop there. It is a place for offerings. It is a place where the physical is made spiritual. The altars fulfill that function. Likewise, the woman's desk is a place for ideas to become real.

The Mishkan enables the physical to dwell next to the spiritual by physically rendering the spiritual and creating a space where the physical (offerings) can be converted into the spiritual. It is an interface. The heroine's Mishkan is an interface, with physical objects representing the revelation of ideas.

Finally, the heroine is the priest of her own tabernacle. She lives with one foot in the world of men and the other in a very different world we can barely understand.

She is the one who enables her Tabernacle to function.

Just like a priest she is not the great leader. She is a specialist, focused on a narrow mission.

She, like the Jewish people, is there to enable creation and innovation while combating fear and uncertainty.

She represents an ideal for a nation of priests and a Holy people.

Tetzaveh: The Secular Kohen

I have to say, I was surprised by the knock on my door. I was living alone, in an old apartment in Petach Tikva. I didn't have many – no scratch that – I *never* had any guests. It wasn't that I was a loner, not at all. It was that I was embarrassed. The apartment had been owned by my parents. I'd inherited it from them, and I'd never really left it. Sure, I went to school and the army and got a job and all that – but I'd always lived there, in that same tiny, run-down apartment. I'd thought about upgrading it now and then, but between the long hours and my low salary as an associate Professor of Fashion Design at the Tel Aviv School of Art, it had never really been possible. If I received packages, I received them at my office at the school. Nobody even came asking for money – a frequent enough occurrence in Israel. My house didn't have a promising look.

Nonetheless, there was that knock. For the first time I could remember, I got up to open the door. On the other side was an old man, a Rabbi, facing me. He was dressed all in black. He was clearly in the wrong neighborhood.

"Sorry," I said, "I don't have money for you." He just stood there and smiled mysteriously. The Haredim had always annoyed me. They sat in Yeshivot and studied while I served in the army, worked and paid my taxes. *I* paid *them* to sit around.

The man kept standing there. "Get a job," I said, roughly, and began to close the door.

"Actually," said the man, "I'd like to offer you a job."

That was enough to stop me from closing the door. What the heck was he talking about?

"Your parents died, in an accident at sea?" he asked, carefully.

"Yes," I said, not wanting to remember their vacation gone horribly wrong.

"And there was no funeral, I mean, with a body?" he asked.

"That's correct," I said slowly. I was beginning to lose my patience.

"Have you ever been to a funeral?" he asked.

"I've never been to a funeral," I shot back, "What the hell is this all about?"

"Well," said the man, with that same calm smile, "That's good. I'm here as a representative of the Sanhedrin."

"Uh," I answered, uncertain, "The Sanhedrin?"

"The famous Rabbinical court?" he said. It was a question. He was almost curious whether I knew what he was talking about. I wanted to yank the man's beard. This had to be a practical joke.

"And what," I asked, "do you want with me?"

"We have appealed to the government, for a dispensation."

"Okay?" I asked.

"We want to temporarily place the Mishkan – the temporary, travel-size, version of the Temple – on the Temple Mount during the three Holiday festivals. We'd displace nothing else; we'd just enable Jewish worship at the site. And because the building is inherently temporary, we'll take it down and move it elsewhere afterwards."

"What does this have to do with me?" I asked.

"For reasons I can't really understand, you've been selected for a critical job."

"What job?" I asked.

"Kohen Gadol," said the man, referring to the role of High Priest.

I just stared at him. And then I did it. I reached out and tugged at his beard. He yelped. The beard didn't come off.

I slowly pulled my hand away. I was a bit embarrassed, but I still couldn't believe this guy was real.

"How could I possibly be the Kohen Gadol?" I asked.

"Because the Sanhedrin has chosen you for the job," said the old man, still wincing.

"But why," I asked, incredulous, "I think the whole Jewish Temple thing is a bunch of dangerous ritualistic mumbo-jumbo."

The Rabbi smiled gently and said, "Consider this an opportunity to learn about a particular culture and type of design."

I just looked at him, less than convinced. But then he added, "We have substantial foreign contributions and are able to offer you a significant stipend."

That got my attention. My apartment needed the help.

"Okay," I said, after a pause that was shorter than my pride would normally have allowed.

I got permission from my department. They saw it as an intense and insider's view of a particular culture of design. I was granted an impromptu Sabbatical; opportunities like this didn't pop up every millennium.

What followed was an extensive training program. It was just what I expected, a whole bunch of mumbo-jumbo. The people who were teaching me all seemed to resent me. They couldn't understand why *I* was chosen. And I got that. The rules seemed to call for somebody wise and full of the fear of G-d – I certainly didn't fit their definition of those words. Heck, I didn't fit my own definition of those words. I firmly belonged to Israel's secular camp. I wasn't committed to *not* believing in G-d – but I was certainly on the spectrum.

I didn't fit what they wanted. And yet, somehow, the Sanhedrin had chosen me. I couldn't begin to understand it.

As I learned, I was shocked by how committed my teachers were. They acted like followers of a mindless cult. They memorized the laws and procedures and yet none of them seemed able to give me a decent explanation for *why* we were studying what we were studying. Why offer up a bull for this procedure or that? Why build this weird little building? Sure, they had nice little homilies for some things. But the whole package never seemed to come together. Everything seemed to have some partial, mystical, take as to *why* even though the *what* was incredibly detailed in its nature. It seemed like a mockery of ritual.

Incredibly, though, I took it all in. I understood the procedures. I memorized them. I could act them out, perfectly, after one mock run. And I was also willing to carry them out. I was remarkably pliable. But I didn't understand them. Of course, it seemed like nobody did.

As we dug deeper, I realized that in many cases the people teaching me didn't understand the *what* either. What do angels on cloth look like? What kind of weaving went into garments? What was the true shape of the Menorah or the angels on the Ark? They didn't know. Nobody knew.

But I was a University Professor. And so, I began to ask around. The Rabbis had their sources and I had mine. It was a fun little project for those I worked with. They weren't committed to any of it either. But, slowly and surely, they began to share what they knew and what they could learn. And slowly and surely, we moved away from the Greek images of Herod's Temple and back towards something far more fundamental. And then, slowly but surely, they got more and more involved. Archeologists, literary critics, industrial designers, sociologists, political scientists – they all found themselves being pulled into this world. A distraction became a passion. Their hearts were poured into the work.

It was during this process, riding on the backs of Rabbis and Professors alike, that I began to understand the symbolism. Some of it was obvious. Blue is the color of sky, a place without loss and death. Purple of honor. But some was less obvious. My University colleagues began to pore over the text – not to discover what was wrong or human or edited in it. But to figure out what was meant by certain terms. They used their tools, their secular tools, to tie things together. The "scarlet red" of Tola'at Shani referred to the worms that ate the Manna. They taught trust in G-d, but also represented His faithfulness to us. The Shiesh Mashzar referred to linen, the fabric equivalent of wheat; grown and processed by man. It represented our labor. And so on and so forth.

Slowly but surely opinions shifted. We went from trying to tear down to trying to understand. And then, slowly but surely, we began to uncover a logic in the text. There was a symbolic logic, hidden right below the surface. Even those who were convinced it was one of the worst-edited documents in history began to see it. They began to see it because, for the first time, they were *looking* for it. Not only that, but they began to educate those who had spent their lives studying it.

All of this went well, our national understanding growing, until we got to the garments of the Kohen Gadol. When we hit the clothes *I* was supposed to wear, we hit a wall.

We knew the materials. We knew the verses, Professors and Rabbis alike. We'd guessed and surmised and tried out ways of making these garments. But we had no idea what they stood for. We'd researched for months. We'd examined other nearby cultures. We dug through the Talmud. But nothing was satisfying. To me, at least, the clothes were a mystery.

During this entire process, the 'sample' Mishkan that had been assembled in Shiloh was being brought up to snuff. Materials were being upgraded, assumptions checked, and patterns woven once again. But finally, the building was ready. It was disassembled and then carried to the entrance of the Temple Mount.

Security was incredibly high. We were going to assemble the Mishkan for one week, and then take it down again. It was to be a week of consecration. The literal word was Chanukah, 'dedication'. And so, Chanukah had been chosen as the time of construction. This was the only time, at least for the foreseeable future, that we'd put the building up on the mount outside of the three pilgrimage festivals.

It was a rainy day, a miserable day. The government security forces were glad of it. It muted the angry crowds just a bit. This was to be an incursion, after all. We were going to establish our central place of prayer in its proper place. And those who did not accept us, who believed they were there to replace us – both on the Temple Mount and in our relationship with G-d – were not pleased.

To the world, this innovation had been cast as a matter of freedom of worship. But it had also been cast as a response. A group of international Jewish visitors had been attacked while visiting the site. Three had been killed. The construction of the Mishkan, even temporarily, was a response to that violence. It was a statement that the Temple Mount of millennia past was *still* the center of Jewish worship.

I was in a small tent to the side of the Mishkan itself. I was there by myself. I was dressed in my normal clothes, but I had gone to the Mikvah – the ritual bath – only a short while before. Water cleanses toxins from our cells and brings nutrients in. I tried to feel that spiritual parallel as I dunked in the waters. But I couldn't find it within me.

And yet, here I was. I could tell you all the offerings that would be made. And I knew, despite all the opprobrium, that I was going to carry so many of them out. I was even beginning to understand the idea of animal sacrifice. If my friends could eat shrink-wrapped cow on the road to work in the morning, and call it moral, I could dedicate the life of an animal to something greater and call it 'holy'. I might not have believed in G-d, but I understood the power of symbols and of design in a society.

Now, now it was time to don the garments and transform myself. I found myself doing something I never expected to do. I prayed. I prayed for understanding.

I disrobed and took the roughly woven linen undergarments from the stack. As I put them on, I understood their purpose. Just as the Rabbis had told me, they were there to cover nakedness.

The undergarments on, some assistants came into the small tent. It was while they dressed me in the basic Kohen's robes that I was blessed with the understanding I had prayed for.

It started with the finely woven and highly patterned linen tunic. As I touched it, I understood it. Made of linen, it represented human creation and effort. If I was to enter the presence of G-d, I was bringing the people's handiwork before Him. Their labor was being dedicated to something timeless and spiritual. I had seen the craftsmen and women pouring their love into this vestment.

Next came the sash. The fabrics in it, I knew, represented G-d's promise to us as well as His purity and honor. When I put it on, I realized that I am making myself more G-dly.

And then came the turban. The hair, grown long in the Nazir, represents human individuality. By covering it, I was minimizing my personal ego – just as the Levi does when he shaves his head.

I knew then that these are the basic roles of the Kohen's clothes. A Kohen is to bring man before G-d and G-d before man and never put himself before the role he must play.

With this in my mind, they continued to dress me, and the ideas expanded within me. The robe, worn only by the Kohen Gadol, came next. It was pure blue, representing the purity of G-d. Even the neckline was not torn – as had once been a common way of making a neckline. The idea of loss is distant to this garment, just as it is distant to G-d. As the robe was lowered over my body I saw the hemline, with its pomegranates and bells. Fruit, in Torah, are always gifts of G-d. These pomegranates are blue, purple and scarlet, capturing His gifts of purity, honor and faithfulness to us. The gold bells on the hemline, I realized, represented G-d's voice. The gold is divine, and hearing is our way of connecting to G-d. A walking man could never control the sound of gold bells on his hem. But G-d could. And the robe has no linen, there is no place for mankind in it.

As it settled over my body, I *knew* this garment was raising me up – making me G-dlike so that I could approach the divine presence and not be erased by its infinity.

The ephod came next. Straps on the ephod come up to my shoulders where the names of the tribes of Israel are engraved on stones and surrounded by gold. I realize the gold once again represents G-d. But here, he is embracing the people. As I walk, I will be carrying the names of the people – embraced by G-d – on my shoulders. The text says it is a reminder (Ex. 28:12). The *ephod* is to remind *me* that I am carrying the relationship between the people and G-d on my shoulders.

The ephod doesn't only have straps over the shoulder. It wraps around me – constraining me. According to most opinions, and the garment I'm wearing matches this, the ephod wraps around the legs. The legs represent *will*, which is why angels are traditionally imagined as having *no* legs. I am constrained by my duty to the relationship between G-d and man.

Like the turban, the ephod constrains my individuality. It replaces my personality with the office of the Kohen Gadol. I could feel this change as well. I was becoming the job.

My assistants then lifted the breastplate of law onto my chest. They connected it to the ephod. The breastplate has the Jewish tribes inscribed on stones. Stones, I know, imply something unchanging and permanent. The stones are connected by materials of purity, honor, divine faithfulness, industry and divinity. And they are embraced by G-d's gold. The tribes are brought together, by G-d. The text says the breastplate is there so that the High Priest can bring the names of the Children of Israel into the place of holiness – continually.

When I wear this breastplate, *I* am bringing the Jewish people, embraced by G-d, into timelessness.

The breastplate comes with two other unique stones, the Urim and Tumim. They roughly translate as 'the enlightened' and 'the perfect'. They represent the law itself, the foundation of our people.

With these garments, my role became stronger. I am to bring the people to G-d.

Finally, the headband was added. It is blue and gold – divine and pure. It says, "Holy to Hashem."

And I realized that it brought everything together. I became a message rather than a man.

I stepped out of that small tent. For a moment, at least, the rain had stopped. But, only meters away, a crowd held back by the police, was shouting abuse at me. They aren't the only ones there, though. I saw the Rabbis there, and the Professors. I saw the curious crowds – separated from the angry Islamic worshippers. Many in that crowd had been drawn by the oddity of this Kohen Gadol. This Kohen Gadol who was secular until just moments before.

I saw the head of the Sanhedrin then, sitting in the center of a collection of Rabbis. I hadn't realized, until just that moment, that he was the man who came to my door. I see him, and he sees me, and he smiles. That same smile.

I realized, just then, *why* I had been chosen.

On my breastplate was the tribe of Shimon. It was a tribe that was not even blessed by Moshe. It was a tribe that went off the road, engaging in acts alien to G-d's people. But *I* carried them, nonetheless. I was not to be Kohen of the religious Zionists or the Haredim. I was to be the Kohen Gadol of *all* the people. I was to bring them all before G-d, and G-d before them.

Adorned with my garments, I felt *myself* drifting away. I felt the presence of G-d in me. I felt the presence of the people. The Professor of Design was gone, at least for the day.

As I brought the offerings, I realized that they too capture this theme. With a bull, which represents a nation, I bring the people to G-d, one of them being offered up at the dedication of Yitzchak by his father. I bring their timebound and physical gifts up to the timeless.

With the rams, I symbolically constrain myself. They represent fear of G-d. I place myself in the first of them, laying my hands on it. And then I dip the blood of the second on my right toe, thumb and ear. I am dedicating the prime of my will (from my legs), my action (from my arms) and my obedience (from my ears), to G-d.

Finally, with the continual offering, I connect this moment to all time. I represent G-d's timeless presence in the here and now. The offering is of a sheep. Shepherding people, with time for poetry and war, have great freedom and little regularity or order. The greatest Jewish leaders are shepherds. And yet, the G-dly is made a part of their wildness.

As they watch, I know the Professors and Rabbis alike begin to understand what is happening. They can see both the divine and the human in my garments and my actions. They can see it in my office.

I am beginning, step by step, offering by offering, to once again sew together the relationships between the Jewish people and their G-d and between the Jewish people themselves.

And that is how I became the secular Kohen Gadol.

Ki-Tisa: The Stadium of Light

Aaron Mizrahi slowly climbed the steps to the stage. He could feel the energy of the crowd around him. There were 40,000 people here. 40,000 people who had come to hear *him* speak. He was blown away by how quickly his world has changed. Less than a year earlier, he'd been a waiter at a café in Jerusalem. Actually, waiter was too fancy a word. So was café. He'd been working the counter at a hole-in-the-wall falafel shop in Talpiot. The shop itself was located in a narrow alley stuffed with mechanics' stalls. There was constant traffic and not a fair bit of honking as the mechanics' customers weaved their way through the mass of parked vehicles. And, of course, everything was covered with the grime and grease of automotive repair.

It was a humble establishment and Aaron didn't even own it. He only worked there, feeding the mechanics' customers falafel and more than a few cups of sludge-like coffee and watching their faces as they bore the burden of automotive expense.

Aaron had had higher aspirations. He'd come out of the army dreaming of a job in high-tech. But, somehow, he failed the psychometric testing that was all the rage in Israel at the time. Something about him didn't fit what the computers and the systems designed to assemble the ideal workforce were seeking. The fact was, he hated the psychometric tests, and he suspected that the tests themselves knew it.

So, he's taken the first job he's found. Working at a bottom-of-the-barrel falafel shop had been convenient. The mechanics' shops weren't far from his parents' house, where he still lived. Having

113

secured that lowly position, he just never left. He worked in that dead-end job for 11 years, going nowhere, slowly.

Then, in under a year, he had climbed to where he is now. He couldn't quite believe it himself.

And, yet, here he was. A stage had been set up at one end of the field in Teddy Stadium. The field and three quarters of the stadium seats (the three quarters that could see the stage) were stuffed with a standing-room-only crowd. And more people were crowded outside, watching huge monitors that had been set up. Hundreds of thousands more were watching on a live online broadcast.

As he took his place at the podium, all these screens shifted. They followed him as he bounded up the stairs. He could feel the millions of eyeballs tracking him. It made him uncomfortable. It wasn't stage fright, it all just seemed *inappropriate* to him.

As he took his place at the podium, a massive cheer rose up through the crowd.

Aaron tried to look out at them. He tried to see the people. They were why he was here. Now, as they assembled, he could feel their power. He had to see them. He had to thank them. He had to acknowledge them.

But he couldn't. The lights were all on him. The crowd was invisible to his eyes.

As he cleared his throat, a hush rippled through the stadium.

And then he spoke.

"To the beloved person who is in charge of the lights..." he paused, and then continued, "Can you shine them on the crowd?"

He sensed movement on the stage and a man hurried up to him, a headset resting on his head. "What?" he whispered.

Aaron turned to him, but spoke through the mic, "Are you in charge of the lights?"

"Yes," said the man, quietly, glancing around.

"And your name is?"

"Amir," said the man.

"This is our beloved Amir," Aaron announced, "And he is charge of the lights."

A cheer rose through the crowd. Amir glanced out, uncertain.

Aaron continued, "I would like him to shine the lights on *you*, the crowd. I would like to see *you* and I would like *you* to see each other."

"And the video?" asked Amir.

"The video too," said Aaron, as hundreds of thousands watched. "Show us the faces of these beloved people."

The tech scurried back off stage.

And then, one-by-one, the lights focused on Aaron went down. And the lights that showed the crowd came up. Aaron could see them now, almost indistinctly small. He turned to look at the monitor, and he saw it too had changed. Instead of focusing on him, the camera was meandering through the crowd. He could see them now, one looking to the other, as if they hadn't noticed their neighbors until now. Now, they noticed each other. He could see introductions and smiles of appreciation. There was a rippled murmuring that trickled through the stadium. It was like electricity for his soul.

"I can feel," he announced, his voice growing in strength, "The love of this crowd."

He saw the faces on the screen craning to see him. But he was far away.

"Do not look to me," he said, trying to build the feeling, "Look to each other. *You* are a community. It is *you* who have brought us

115

together. Look to your neighbors. And love them as you love yourself."

The power of the place grew.

"A year ago," said Aaron, his voice reverberating in the open spaces, "I was a serving falafel on mechanics row in Talpiot."

The crowd roared. And Aaron listened. And felt.

When it had quieted down, he continued. He continued with a story that every person in the crowd already knew. He had no script, he just felt what the crowd wanted and delivered it to them.

"A man came into my shop. A beloved man. A courier. He owned his own truck. But he had fallen into debt. And now, his truck had broken down. He came into the shop. And I could see the tears on his face. I could see the desperation. I made him a coffee and he sat at the single table. And I sat across from him. And I asked him, 'What has happened?' And he told me his story. And, I don't know why, but I reached for the *kupat tzedakah*, the charity box, on the counter. And I told him, give some money to charity.

"The man looked at me, incredulous. 'I am poor, and in debt and I don't know how I will pay for the repairs to my truck. I don't know how I will live. And you want me to give charity.' I looked at him and then, for a reason I still can't understand, I said, 'Yes.'

"And so, the man gave, just a shekel. But we both felt the effects. There was an energy, a power, that came from that gift. I could see it in the man's face. It was like a world had opened up for him. It was like he could see how wondrous and immense G-d's universe is. But, instead of being diminished, he could sense how beloved he was in that universe. So could I. He didn't leave the coffee shop any richer, materially. But he left far richer in a far more important way.

116

"Soon, more and more of you came. That *kupat tzedakah* filled up. And a light seemed to emanate from the mechanics' alley. It was a grungy place. A place where people faced tremendous financial hardship. But it was also a place where they gave small gifts and reaped incredible rewards.

"It was not long before I discovered this power followed me. In a café, a real café, the same thing would happen. When I prayed in synagogue the daily gifts of charity would shoot an energy into the place. I could enable physical contributions to become spiritual reality. And so, I began to travel the country, sharing this power. I began to travel, helping everyone understand how beloved they are. How connected they can be to the spiritual universe around us.

"Because of this gift, our nation felt more connected than we never had before.

"Then, three months ago, our neighbors launched a coordinated attack on our country. Terrorists in the Sinai assaulted our border fence. Those in Gaza launched rockets. Missiles rained in from Syria and Lebanon. For three months now, the assaults have not stopped. Thousands have died. We have struck back with overwhelming force. Tens of thousands of our enemies have fallen. Yet the war continues. The international community pours malice down on us, condemning us for our defense. All of you, who had felt so connected only months ago, now feel abandoned and alone.

"This is why we have come together. This is why, despite the threat of continual attack, tens of thousands of us have gathered together, in one place. You called me, you organized yourselves, and you asked me to help find you rescue and refuge. And I, I can feel your energy. I can feel the power of this crowd. I can sense the spiritual force within it."

Aaron paused and took a drink from his water. He felt the energy of the place crackling over him. He knew what he had to say.

"We feel abandoned. In the aftermath of our great awakening, we feel abandoned. You feel abandoned. But we do not need to be abandoned. I can feel the power of this community. I can feel the power of this people. We need only look at our history to recognize this power. *We* organized and acted and survived the terror of Europe. *We* organized and acted and built a State in a wasteland. *We* did this. *We* redeemed ourselves from the lowest terrors and the darkest realities. And *we* lifted ourselves up. *We* did it. *We* did it with our Kibbutzim. *We* did it with our army. *We* did it with our culture. *We* did it, with each other. By discovering and unlocking the power of our community."

Aaron tugged at his ear. "This is the power. The power to hear your fellow. The power to *listen* to your fellow. The power to understand that *each* of us is beloved to *all* of us. This power has only grown. Our country has discovered the power of the Internet and social media. *We* help others listen to one another and we have helped form a global community. A community tied together like none before it. A community, a force, a power, that is beyond compare. It is this power that grants so many of us our livelihood. In a land without natural resources, *we* have unlocked the power of *human* resources. The power of our people.

"Because of this, we need not fear. These rockets are but a pinprick. Over 12,000 Jews were killed in a single day in Auschwitz. But *we* overcame that. *We* can overcome this. They will not penetrate our borders; they will only rain fire on us from above. *We* will overcome *them*."

He paused and the crowd roared. They were caught up in the power of the moment. Then Aaron continued.

"Every one of us is connected to billions of others through our phones. They are the ears of today. And the ears of tomorrow. They are the enabler of our collective power. They pull us together into something greater than we have ever envisioned before."

Aaron didn't know what he would say next. Then the strangest idea struck him.

"Amir," he said, "Turn off the lights."

Amir didn't ask questions this time. In a moment, the stadium was cast into darkness. The screen behind him went dark.

Aaron continued, "We do not adorn our phones, but perhaps they can adorn us. Turn your phones on. Turn your cameras on. Point the screens towards me, but cast your cameras on yourselves, use the lights of your phones to illuminate yourselves. Shine a video of yourselves onto this stage. Somehow, we will create an amalgam of our people."

Aaron watched as the crowd complied. He watched as the tiny screens lit up. As the tiny images of people's faces appeared on their many phones and those images shone towards him. Behind him the giant monitor picked up their faces, illuminated by their cell phone lights. Tens of thousands of people, sharing a vision of themselves.

As Aaron watched, he felt the old power surge through him. He saw the images and the lights coalesce in the center of the field. He saw a strange pulsating orb of light hovering over the stadium. He could feel that *he* was creating it. Just as he had taken the physical and made it spiritual, now he was taking the spiritual – the power of the community – and making it physical.

The event cameras shifted. They shifted from the people to the amalgam the people had created. They shifted to that glowing orb of energy. The orb hovered before Aaron himself.

Spontaneously, the people began to dance. They began to sway and move. He could feel them, looking one to another, with love and respect.

Aaron began to chant. "*We* are the power. *We* have redeemed ourselves. And *we* will redeem ourselves once again."

He repeated himself. "*We* are the power. *We* have redeemed ourselves. And *we* will redeem ourselves again."

The chant was picked up in the crowd. It grew and crackled. The shouting grew louder, the chant more insistent. The glowing mass above the field grew ever brighter. There was power in a crowd, there was power in *this* community.

"Celebrate yourselves!" Aaron shouted over the joyful noise.

He could hear that they did. He could hear them worshipping their community and rewarding themselves in their joyful redemption. The rockets were but an annoyance in the face of *this* power.

Aaron just closed his eyes and listened. He had hated the psychometric software because it sucked the spiritual from the human. But here he was, placing the human into the spiritual. He closed his eyes, and he felt the power of the community.

How could they not worship such power?

--

But G-d was watching. G-d was listening. And G-d was remembering. Thousands of years before, this same people had taken their gold earrings and made a G-d of their community. It was an amalgamated golden calf. The calf was the symbol of a young nation. And the gold a sign of its divinity. The gold had coalesced into an idol representing the community itself. It formed itself because the power of the community was real. The people had praised the calf, themselves, for their redemption from Egypt. They had worshipped it by playing.

That was when it was clear they were worshipping themselves.

Aaron, the brother of Moshe, had filled them with the conceit of Pharaoh (Ex 32:25).

Moshe had responded by rending the community apart (Ex. 32:27). Turning brother against brother.

G-d had wanted to destroy them then. G-d had wanted to create them anew. He had wanted to fix their flaw; to replace their core. But Moshe had intervened, and the people had been saved. They had been shown the face of G-d in the attributes that defined His future.

It had come at a cost to the people. Forever more, they would be a bellwether. They would be blessed when they recognized Him. And they would be cursed when they did not. Whether blessed or cursed, the fortunes of this people would forever be a sign of G-d's presence.

G-d wanted the people blessed. But they did not learn. Again and again, G-d had given them the opportunity to understand their own powerlessness and thus recognize the source of their redemption. But, whenever they tasted the fat of His blessings, they found a way to ascribe their redemption to themselves. Despite the thousands of years that had passed, they had never learned.

Now, another Aaron – another man with the power to convert the physical to the spiritual – was repeating the same ancient mistakes.

G-d had promised not to change them, and so even He, the all-powerful one, had simply to hope that His people would learn. They *were to be a bellwether. As Moshe had demanded, they were to be a bellwether. They were to be, through blessings or curses, the evidence of G-d's place in this world.*

They were worshipping themselves once again. And so, they had to be punished.

They had to be punished or the world would never come to recognize the divine.

Vayakel-Pekudai: The House of Love

I sit on a plastic folding chair, looking at the flat concrete slab I've created. As I sit there, I wonder whether she'll ever come back again.

It had all started in an alley. I'd been like some cliché, literally sleeping in that alley. I'd been at the end of the line. I'd reached the bottom, but there was no bounce waiting for me. I wasn't going to get back up.

I wasn't some uneducated classless teenager who just fell into drugs because I had nothing else to do. I'd grown up in a solid family and although I wasn't brilliant, I'd been an excellent student. I managed it by working harder than everybody around me. In the end, that had been what had undone me.

Somehow, I'd managed to get into John Hopkins Medical School after college. That was where things began to go wrong. My first semester of Biochem had been the problem. I got a 'B' in the first exam. That wouldn't have been the end of the world, but I could feel the material slipping through my fingers. My grades were going to get worse.

I upped my effort. I began to drink more and more coffee. I switched to energy drinks. Soon, I graduated to caffeine pills. It wasn't enough. I couldn't keep up. I got a 'C' on my second test. I knew where this was going. I knew myself. I wasn't bright enough to catch up once I'd fallen behind. I would, inexorably, end up failing the course. I would drop out and I would end up losing everything I'd worked so hard to achieve.

I needed another level.

I turned to meth.

The results were immediate. I could stay up longer and work harder. I got a remarkable amount done. I reversed my downward slide and passed the course. My grades weren't perfect, I got a 'B'. My professor said he was tremendously surprised by the reversal. Very few students manage it. Plus, everybody said that first semester of Biochem was the hardest. I'd done it. Having passed that hurdle, I could just back off the meth, go back to my coffee and get back to my life.

It wasn't that easy. I had tremendous will power, I knew it. What I didn't have was *time*. I tried to come off the meth, cold turkey, but the impact was overwhelming. *Everything* went wrong. I found myself paranoid, panicked and literally hallucinating. My entire body ached, and I was exhausted; I couldn't stop sleeping. I was going to fail school and drop out – *because* I was coming off the meth. I didn't have a choice, I stayed on. I hoped a long break would give me the time I needed to quit. The gaps between semesters were never long enough, though. It didn't help that the almost sweet smell of meth seemed to speak to my soul – calling me back whenever I thought about trying to quit, again.

School, of course, got harder. The benefits of the drug retreated. Things just kept getting worse and worse. I found myself failing despite it all. I was falling apart, and my body was aging at an incredible rate. I flunked out of school, and I just kept falling. Eventually, I found myself sleeping in an alley and stumbling out in the day to look for some money and another hit. I knew I didn't have long, and I knew there was nothing I could do about it.

Then, she showed up. She was like an angel. Her face was radiant. She was stunningly beautiful. And she was coming into the lowliness of *my* world. At first, I'd been scared. Somebody like that, coming to me, promised some sort of sick abuse. She didn't push me though. She just offered me a coffee and a smile. She didn't shrink from me; she was willing to talk to me. She was willing to listen. Most importantly, she could understand me.

It must have been a week or two before she finally got me to come out of the alley with her. She brought me to a restaurant – not just a fast-food place, but a real restaurant. A fancy restaurant. And we had a meal together. She kept helping me. She got me a place in a detox facility. She paid for a whole row of implants to replace my broken teeth. She put more and more trust in me. She rented me a room at a nice hotel. She took care of me. And I rewarded her, in a way. I could still work. I could still put in effort. So, I did. I got off the drugs and I stayed off the drugs. I began to step everything else up too. I wasn't at risk of using again. That was a mistake I wouldn't make a second time.

She also gave me money. Not a few thousand dollars, but a few million. I don't know where she got it and I did care. One day, she just brought me to the bank, helped me open an account and transferred the funds. Just like that, I was a wealthy man. It was like (with the exception of my lack of a medical degree) everything in my life had gone perfectly. I could forget the pain of my fall.

That was the day I decided to buy *us* a gift. I went to the dealership and bought a car. Specifically, I bought a Lexus LC500, a beautiful, classy, two-door coupe. We could drive in it, together – wrapped in leather and luxury and style. I brought it to her, presented to her and waited for her response. She smiled appreciatively, but something was missing. It hadn't been what she'd wanted.

Then she brought me to her house. Until that day, I hadn't even noticed I'd never been to her house. I knew nothing about her. But there it was. It was a perfectly proportioned little blue home, like a patch of the sky planted on the side of a suburban street. She invited me in and then showed me plans. They were blueprints for another house and the furniture that would go in it. As I looked them over, I realized the plans were for a house that celebrated our strange relationship. It was a tiny house. But every detail was covered. There was a coffee machine, an odd detail for house plans. There was a table, just like that at the fancy restaurant. There was a fireplace, tremendously unusual in a place so small, and there was a couch in front of it. It was a place where we could be together, basking in the warmth of our relationship. The house was like a little temple. There was a place outside the front door for shoes, like you'd find in Japan. And there was a small washbasin there as well, where influences of the outside world could be washed from our hands.

She asked me to build it. I agreed. I was delighted with the opportunity.

I started work immediately. I couldn't build the house right away, of course. I had to study. I studied laying a foundation. I bought a truck to haul supplies and I rented a small tractor. I started to smooth and flatten the earth below where the house would be. I felt myself accomplishing something for the first time since medical school. As I finished the grading and began to pour the concrete, a question began to eat at me. I couldn't possibly deserve her, could I?

Next, I studied framing, woodworking, electrical wiring, plumbing and more. I worked hard and I learned. I was still bright. I was still capable. I was still hard working. As I progressed, my question changed. Instead of wondering why she'd chosen me, I wondered how I had *earned* her.

As I bought supplies, my question began to turn into an answer. A simple answer: *I had earned her*. It was my dedication, my hard work, my character. It was my mind. I had been the key. The idea grew in me.

Before long, I was certain that I had earned her and that she, somehow, been only the *means* of my redemption.

It was fate, my fate, which had brought her to me.

If not for her, I would have found rescue from another. That was why I added to the design of the house. Just one thing. I painted a portrait, a small portrait, of myself.

That was then she began to withdraw from my life.

Day by day, I saw less and less of her. The money remained, but she didn't. By the time the foundation had cured, the relationship the house had been built to celebrate was gone.

Now, as I look at the empty slab of concrete, I find myself shattered by her absence. There is no fire anymore. None of what I have seems to matter. I'm not on meth, but I have no reason to stay clean. I have everything, but I am somehow completely without purpose or hope.

As I sit there, lost, I suddenly realize the key to my questions. She was beautiful, and smart and wealthy. Any man, any successful man, couldn't help but somehow think that they'd *earned* her. They couldn't help but be proud, tremendously proud, of the woman they had 'acquired'. Before long, they would have grown convinced she had chosen them because of how remarkable they were. To think otherwise would be to acknowledge their own tremendous limitations. Their thoughts, their attitudes, would poison the relationship she was seeking. Their need for *self* would undermine everything.

That's why she'd chosen me. I'd been nothing. Rising from that alley, there was no way I could possibly think I'd earned *anything*. And, yet, I had. I'd gone so far as to even paint a portrait of myself. I'd celebrated me in preference to her.

So, she'd left.

The house is far from done. Nonetheless, I take the truck, buy some bricks, and begin to assemble the fireplace *she* had planned. Then I set a fire in it, in the center of this non-existent building. The fire started, I begin to work around it, building everything to plan. I work deliberately, slowly, with love. I single-handedly put up the walls and paint them. I work with the wood I'd carefully sourced to create the table she had specified. Bit by bit, the house comes together. Constantly, the fire burns. It is a constant reminder of why I am building the house. As I work, the house begins to represent more than our relationship. Instead, every beam, every panel, every nail, speaks of my dedication to that relationship.

I imagine her watching me, from far away. I never see her, though. I just keep working, hoping she'll appear. And, constantly, that fire burns.

When I am almost done, I take the portrait I'd commissioned, and I throw it into the fire. Minutes later, I collect the ashes and cast them into glass bowls; glass basins in which I can wash my hands when I come into this house. I will cleanse my hands with my regret.

Finally, the house is done. A small, perfect house. A house I have poured my heart into.

But it is a house that is still missing what it needs most.

It is a house that is still missing *her*.

I sit on the front step, just waiting and hoping she'll appear. And then she does. She is walking towards me. She is like an angel. She is stunningly beautiful. Radiant. She is once again coming into the lowliness of my world.

We sit before the fire and in that moment, I know why I have been chosen. I know why she'd left. And I know, somehow, that she'll always come back again.

--

The first description of the Mishkan comes in the shadow of the people's inappropriate shared sacrifice of bulls and building of pillars. It restricts us to an appropriate form of worship.

The second description comes after the sin of the calf. It comes after Moshe reminds us that we cannot have fire in our homes on Shabbat. Fire represents spiritual energy. Without the Mishkan, we are missing the flame of Hashem that should be yielded by our investment in our divine relationship.

The second description captures the emotional process of relighting the flame of our relationship. We can see this emphasis in the details.

In the first description, the incense altar comes well after the copper altar. Incense, smell, speaks to emotion while the copper altar represents the practical process of investing in the divine relationship. In the first telling, emotion comes well after investment. But with the second telling, the order is reversed. The golden altar comes first; emotion leads to investment.

In the second telling, we build the walls, representing our desire to embrace G-d, before the articles – which represent His revelations to us.

In the second telling, we see eager, noble hearts and an excess of giving throughout the process. The people are emotionally investing in rebuilding their relationship with G-d.

And, in the second telling, we see how the gold in the Kohen Gadol's garment is beaten flat and then cut into threads. The Kohan Gadol is restricted and cut back in his representation of G-d. He is humbled because of the mistake he made. In addition, the regular sash has its materials defined, showing how the regular Kohanim are wrapped and restricted by the attributes of Hashem.

But the most revealing change is that of the washbasins. In the first telling, the washbasins were described contiguously to the anonymous donations of the half-shekel (Ex. 30:17). It seems the priests are to cleanse themselves of any individual influences. They cleanse themselves of humanity. But in the second telling, those washbasins are made from women's mirrors (Ex. 38:8). The women are described as a multitude – recalling the masses of the people who worshipped the calf. The tools of vanity that led to self-worship are sacrificed to prepare the Kohanim for their proximity to G-d. The Kohanim wash their hands in our regret.

In the second telling, we are never commanded to build the Mishkan. We do it because we miss G-d's fire. We build, precisely, to G-d's design – to show our regret at our rebellion and to show our desire for reunification. Through changes in priority, in the order of building, everything is recast. It moves from being a divine expression of love for the people to becoming a human expression of love for the divine.

It is only after everything is complete, at the end of the book of Shemot, that the fire of the Lord comes and dwells within the people (Ex. 40:34).

With that, the repair is complete, and the absence of G-d is corrected. Once again, we can enjoy the presence of G-d's fire on Shabbat.

Author's Note

The Biblical Joseph was given *useful* interpretations when he gave credit to Hashem for his understanding. He finally gave full credit to G-d when he said:

בלעדי: אלקים יענה

"It is not in me, G-d will answer."

I am not a scholar. Instead, I often finding myself asking Hashem for an answer to difficult questions. Almost invariably, a little while later, I find the answer I need, and it becomes a part of what I share and what I write.

I don't think this is anything unusual. I believe *all of us* can do this. We just have to be open to asking, and then be ready to listen to the answers we are given.

Joseph Cox lives in Modiin, Israel and is blessed with a wonderful wife and six children. If this book added to your life, do someone else a favor and share it. Also, *please please* add a review online. It makes an enormous difference.

That's me!

Other Books by the Author

Adult Fiction

The City on the Heights (a novel)

Candidate Everyone

The Hidden Agent

The Boulevard, Torah Shorts Volume 2

The Assessors, Torah Shorts Volume 3

Pete and the Felon, Torah Shorts Volume 4

The Barn, Torah Shorts Volume 5

Children's Fiction

Grobar and the Mind Control Potion

Squiggles and the Pit of Destruction

Other Books by the Author

www.ingramcontent.com/pod-product-compliance
Lightning Source LLC
Chambersburg PA
CBHW021922170626
46807CB00007B/2936